'You're my woman, Avon

To motherless Avon N and travelling West to live wild state of Montana i passenger Ken Grant to escape possibly unjust punishment is no more than she would have done for anyone in trouble.

Not realising the repercussions of that encounter, she soon settles to her new life on her uncle's farm. But she cannot forget the man met so fleetingly—a man she discovers is branded as a killer and is now a fugitive hiding deep in the lonely hills, determined to prove his innocence. Avon is sure he will get what he wants—and he had said quite definitely that he wanted her!

Man from Montana

Ann Edgeworth

MILLS & BOON LIMITED
London · Sydney · Toronto

First published in Great Britain 1982
by Mills & Boon Limited, 15–16 Brooks Mews,
London W1A 1DR

© Ann Edgeworth 1982
Australian copyright 1982
Philippine copyright 1982

ISBN 0 263 74101 X

Set in 10 on 10½pt Linotron Times
04/1282

Photoset by Rowland Phototypesetting Ltd
Bury St Edmunds, Suffolk
Made and printed in Great Britain by
Cox & Wyman Ltd, Reading

CHAPTER
ONE

It had become unbearably hot. The late afternoon sun that was splashing its golden splendour over the country-side made a furnace of the slowly moving train, and the air coming in the window beside Avon Meredith was as hot as that inside the swaying coach where a few passengers lolled in sleep.

Avon took off her bonnet and wiped her hot forehead and longed for the weary journey to end. She glanced at the little enamelled watch pinned to the bodice of her dress, the only thing she had to remind her of her mother who had died a year ago, and hoped she would get to Miles City before twilight, if twilight—that gentle dove-grey melting of day into night that England knew—ever came to this harsh, wide Montana country with its blazing sunlight and velvet, star-studded nights.

She looked out of the window, but the brilliant light hurt her eyes and she turned her glance to the tall, rangy, deeply tanned man sleeping opposite her. He had removed his hat and nodded to her before replacing it when he entered the coach earlier in the day, and he had got down her holdall when she wished to get a book from it and had made a few remarks on the heat, to which she had answered briefly and coolly. She had become accustomed to travelling alone on the long trip from England and had learned to discourage the approach of men whose eyes brightened when they saw her. Not that the sleeping man's eyes had expressed interest, they were a cold, vivid blue and his expression was uncompromisingly stern, almost forbidding, and he had folded his arms, pulled his wide hat over his forehead and almost at once dropped into sleep.

She sighed, and pulled the neck of her dress away from her hot skin, wishing she had thought to wear something thinner. Her step-mother had given her a striped muslin dress, simple in design and suitable for life on a farm, which would have been better. It had been the only present her step-mother had ever given her and had been prompted, Avon knew, by feelings of relief and guilt: relief that a pretty, high-spirited step-daughter who put a step-sister in the shade was leaving a home where she was no longer welcome, and guilt that Avon's weak, selfish father had so easily been bullied into sending his motherless daughter to live with his brother who had been settled on a small farm in Montana for many years. The Merediths had lost a daughter five years ago and when approached, Ben Meredith had written agreeing to give his niece a home. His wife had not written.

Avon's thoughts were bitter as she recalled her step-mother's antagonism and her father's hurtful complaisance at parting with his only child so easily. A year after his wife's death he had married a wealthy widow with a daughter the same age as Avon, a pale nervous girl eclipsed by Avon's vivid beauty and sparkling personality. The new Mrs Meredith had no intention of having her daughter's chances spoiled and soon made it plain she would not accept a step-daughter.

'And so I am being sent as far as possible,' Avon thought wryly as she braced herself against the swaying of the train. 'Uncle Ben has agreed to take me but he may not truly want me—and he has said nothing of Aunt Rita or what *her* feelings are about me.'

With an effort she pulled her thoughts away from the past year, with its sorrow of losing a mother she loved, a gentle woman who had named her daughter after a river in her beloved Warwickshire, and turned to the window to see the train slackening its pace. As she peered out, the man opposite opened his eyes and said,

'There's a sharp curve ahead . . .' He stopped abruptly as a fusillade of shots rang out and the train jerked to a sudden halt, flinging Avon forward out of her seat. She would have fallen if the man had not caught and held her.

'What is it?' she cried anxiously. 'What has happened? Why have we stopped?'

'Rest easy, Ma'am, and just stay here quiet and peaceful and they won't bother you none.'

'But who . . . what . . .' She clutched his arm as she heard more shots and shouting.

'I guess it's some gents that have their eyes on the express car,' he spoke easily, still holding her, but she saw his lips tighten as he glanced out of the window. 'Reckon we must be toting bankstock or maybe wages for the mines.'

'You mean—train robbers?' she gasped.

'That's right, Ma'am. It's their favourite trick, catching a train as she slows up for a bend. They'll bust open the express wagon and take what they're after and rattle their hocks mighty quick after. Ain't nothing to scare you, Ma'am.'

Avon drew herself out of his arms and sank back in her seat.

'I am not in the least scared! I just think it is disgraceful that such a thing can happen.' Shouts from outside startled her. The other passengers rose hurriedly. A woman screamed and a man snapped:

'Best do what the bastard says an' get out!'

As Avon rose, her fellow passenger caught her arm, holding her back.

'Don't worry to get out, they won't stay long. They'll makė for a quick getaway—' He broke off abruptly as the door of the coach was jerked open and a man wearing a black mask and holding a gun, snapped,

'Drop yore gun an' reach for the sky!'

The tall man hesitated, then obeyed. As his gun fell to the floor the bandit leaped into the coach and caught it up. His eyes went to Avon who was staring at him.

'Well, if you don't have a mighty purty lady friend! Mebbe she'll give me that nice little watch she's wearing —an' a kiss to go with it!'

Avon shrank back as he came towards her, cold with horror.

The tall man started forward, sudden fire in his eyes. 'You get the hell out of here!'

The robber swung around with a curse and aimed his gun deliberately.

'Guess you got this coming to you, stranger!' As his finger tightened on the trigger, Avon sprang forward and knocked his hand up, sending the bullet through the coach roof. Before the man could recover, the tall man lunged and his fist smashed into the robber's masked face. The mask slipped and Avon saw an ugly purple birthmark across one cheek just as shots rang out and a warning yell came from the men outside. The robber scrambled to his feet, cursing, and blundered to the door and ran to a group of mounted men. In a minute he had flung himself on a horse and the whole gang rode off, leaving the group of pale-faced passengers staring after them.

Avon sank onto a seat as a momentary faintness seized her. Her heart was beating wildly and she was trembling. Suddenly a flask was thrust into her hand.

'Drink some of this.'

'Oh no . . . I couldn't.'

'Drink it, it'll steady you.' The command startled her into choking down a few sips of the fiery spirit.

'Have they gone?' she asked fearfully.

'Yep, they got what they were after, I reckon.' He was at the door and, revived by the raw whiskey, she joined him and saw a group of passengers standing around two men lying on the ground beside the engine.

'I shall find out what has happened,' she said firmly and stepped down onto the rough grass beside the track. She expected the man to follow her but he retreated into the coach as she walked to the little group. One of the men on the ground was bleeding from a wound in his shoulder and the other man had a head wound and had fainted.

A woman holding two small children told her the outlaws had attacked both the engineer and the fireman when the train halted, and had burst open the express car and taken the Wells Fargo box from it.

'I guess them two fellows ain't in no way to drive a train now,' she said. 'The men have gone to a farm for horses so's they can ride to Miles City for a spare engineer, and for the sheriff. It ain't but about three miles off.'

'And the robbers have got away!' Avon exclaimed, her grey eyes flashing.

'Lucky they did, 'fore they done more damage,' the woman said. 'Last time there was a hold-up on the line, two men got shot dead.' She turned away. 'Reckon we're stuck here till evening.'

Avon walked slowly back to her coach after seeing both injured men were alive and being attended to. She was still shaken by what had happened. It was a raw beginning to her life in this wide, untamed country. Her fellow passenger helped her into the coach and she told him what she had heard.

'They have sent for another man to drive the train, and for the sheriff. Perhaps he will catch the thieves.' She paused, struck by a change in the man's expression as he moved to the far side of the coach and peered out of the window. He turned and stood looking at her intently, his thumbs hooked into the waistband of his pants.

'I reckon you saved my life, Miss Meredith,' he said slowly, 'and I'm saying thank you—and I won't forget it.' A sudden grin creased his lean brown cheeks, softening the severity of his face. 'For a lady from England you sure moved fast and furious.'

'I—I was afraid he would kill you,' she stammered, disconcerted by something she saw in his face.

'I'm sure glad he didn't,' he drawled, 'or mebbe I'd never have had—this!'

Before she could move or be aware of his intention, he had caught her in his arms, imprisoning her against his hard body while he kissed her with a harsh intensity that made her head swim and her heart beat wildly.

He released her as abruptly as he had caught her, and as she staggered back, too startled and furious to find words, he slid open the door on the far side and, after a swift glance to right and left, dropped onto the bank and raced across the ground and into a group of trees. From there the ground dropped away into a narrow valley and she saw him no more.

Her hands flew to her burning cheeks as she stared after him. How *dared* he! She could still feel the strength of his arms and her mouth seemed to burn from his kisses. Who was he? And why had he left the train so furtively? All the passengers were clustered around the injured men on the other side and could not be aware anyone had left the coach. What had driven him off so abruptly to hide in a belt of trees like a hunted man?

Suddenly she remembered the wary look on his face when she told him some men had ridden to fetch the sheriff from Miles City. Was that his reason for leaving? Could he be in league with the bandits, perhaps a spy who boarded the train to discover what valuables it carried? But the masked man would surely not turn his gun on a confederate?

She waited for her heart to cease pounding, then smoothed her hair, put on her bonnet and shook out her skirts before catching up her reticule. As she left the coach she noticed the label dangling from her holdall on the rack. So that was how he had learned her name.

'Ain't nothing to do but wait for the sheriff and the engineer,' a man told her as she joined the other passengers. 'Mebbe we'll get to the city before dark.'

'Will the sheriff chase the robbers?'

'Likely he will, though they've a head start and mebbe

will cache their haul someplace.' He rubbed a finger across his unshaven chin. 'My guess is they're part of the gang that's been busy in the state. Bank robberies and such. They work fast and get away prompt.'

'Surely the law should do something?'

He shrugged. 'The law ain't catched up with the Blackface gang yet and ain't likely to. They're no beginners in the game, there's some mighty clever brains planning their raids.'

'They always wear black masks?'

He nodded. 'No one ain't seen their faces as I know of. They got their spies and know when to raid.'

The tall man had not looked like a spy.

'But I don't know what a spy does look like,' she thought as she went back to her coach. 'If he *was* one, why didn't he ride away with the gang?'

The woman with the two children was having trouble keeping them in order. Avon joined her and took one of the hot, restless little boys on her knee and kept him amused by telling him stories.

'What size is Miles City?' she asked the woman.

'Well, it don't look much from the train; I guess it's pretty small. Me, I'm going further west.'

The time dragged wearily. But as the sun sank, the heat began to leave the wide rolling plains and Avon, strolling to and fro in the shade of a clump of cottonwoods, felt a breeze cool her hot cheeks. Suddenly she heard a shout, and looked up swiftly as a group of horsemen came riding towards the train. She ran forward eagerly and saw a big man with a star pinned on his shirt swing himself down from his horse to be surrounded by a vociferous crowd. His companions went to examine the smashed door of the express car while others bent over tracks left by the robbers.

'Ain't much to go on,' Avon heard a man say. 'Same gang as held up the train two months ago, I guess. Black masks and quick work. They knew what they wanted to get. You'll trail 'em, Haskin?'

The big man nodded. 'Just as soon as I've asked a few questions.' He turned to the crowd. 'Anyone seen a tall young fellow with blue eyes and a kind of hard manner on the train?' Avon gave a start and felt her nerves tighten. 'Could have boarded the train some ways back.'

'There was a young fellow sitting right at the back, by the young lady,' a woman volunteered. The sheriff turned as she pointed to Avon.

'Did you notice him, Ma'am?' he asked brusquely.

'I—well no, I'm afraid I didn't, officer,' the words seemed to come of their own accord, before she could think. 'He was sleeping with his hat over his face.'

'Did you take note of anything about him, if he acted restless or kind of scary?'

She shook her head. 'I slept quite a lot myself, or I was reading.'

'D'you see him here?' He indicated the group of passengers.

She pretended to scan the group, then shook her head. 'I don't see him.'

'I guess he could of slipped out at a tank town along the line. You're from England I guess, Ma'am. Travelling far?'

'To Miles City where my uncle, Mr Ben Meredith, will meet me.'

'He's waiting for you at the depot, I was with him when I got news of the hold-up.' The sheriff's eyes were suddenly friendly. 'Ben told me he'd a niece coming to live with him and Rita. I reckon you haven't had a good impression of our country so far, Miss Meredith.' He turned to wave at his men. 'We'll split, boys, but we're too late to do much. As sure as hell they'll either cache the stuff or hole up in the hills.' He nodded to Avon and strode to where a man held his horse. In a few minutes the two groups of horsemen had ridden off and passengers began to straggle back into the train.

The train shuddered, jerked and slowly moved off. Avon, watching shadows lengthening over the flat plains, occasionally broken by ranges of hills and weirdly shaped buttes, was suddenly afraid. What sort of life was she coming to in this unknown land with its endless plains and wide horizons and lawless people? England, rich and peaceful under Queen Victoria, seemed another world, a world she knew and loved—and longed for now as hot tears stung her eyes. Why had she not defied her father and step-mother and refused to leave the country and life she knew? Surely she could have found some type of work, a governess, perhaps, or companion to an invalid or elderly woman.

The train had rounded the bend and was gathering speed. Evening was closing in and the dying sun splashed the horizon with a glorious panoply of colour that made Avon catch her breath. Shadows carved the land into gullies and marked out hills rising abruptly from the grasslands. A willow-bordered creek ran for a time beside the track, reflecting the light from the sky. There was a beauty here, disturbing, almost frightening in its vastness and emptiness, but it had a strange magic as she gazed, Avon knew she did not regret escaping the weary life of being an ill-paid and despised employee in England.

She brushed her tears away and sat up, feeling confidence return in a rush of tingling excitement and expectation. Whatever lay before her, she would make the best of it. She was strong, healthy and well educated, and she would try hard to please her aunt and uncle, and when the strangeness had worn off, perhaps she would learn to love this wild unbroken land.

It was true she had been through an unnerving experience. Her train had been held up and robbed, and a mysterious young man with astonishingly blue eyes whose life she had saved had kissed her in a most ungentlemanly manner before escaping the law. She wondered why the sheriff had asked about him, and why, after he had behaved so disgracefully, she had stayed silent about her fellow passenger and pretended she had not seen him disappear.

'I can think nothing good of him,' she thought, 'but he didn't *look* a criminal—and he tried to stop an armed man stealing my watch. Perhaps he hasn't done anything very wrong, or at least, nothing very important.'

The train's pace had slackened and a few small houses slid past the window. Lights showed and passengers began collecting luggage and children as the train pulled into a depot consisting of one long wooden building, a railed-in enclosure for animals, and a cinder path alongside the track.

A group of people were waiting and as Avon stepped down from her coach, a short, thickset man with grey hair came forward and took the holdall she carried.

'Guess you'll be my niece, Avon,' he said awkwardly. 'I'm your Uncle Ben. Reckon you met with a bit of trouble. Were you scared?'

'Well, yes I was, Uncle Ben.' She smiled tentatively at him but got no answering smile. Her uncle's face had a weathered sternness and his manner was formal although not unfriendly. 'I'm sorry you had to wait so long.'

He nodded and called the porter to take the rest of her luggage along the cinder track to where horses and buggies were hitched. As they passed the wooden building that was store house and ticket office, a face on a poster on the wall seemed to leap out at her, a face she knew, young, lean and stern. Beneath it was written: 'Wanted for murder! Ken Grant. Six feet one. Blue eyes and brown hair. Reward!'

CHAPTER
TWO

THE Meredith's farm was a small one. Ben Meredith had emigrated to America in hopes of becoming a rancher with a wide spread of land and good herds of Herefords and Aberdeen Angus's, but bad luck had followed him and, ignorant of the business of ranching, he had been sold bad land for grazing and been duped by unscrupulous men and had lost most of his money. He had bought a piece of land suitable for farming, built a house, married, and resigned himself to a life of hard and, when the weather played tricks, unproductive, work.

As he drove the shabby little one-horse buggy along a road still rutted from spring rains, Ben said abruptly,

'You'll maybe find Rita a little stiff, but don't let it worry you. I told your father I would give you a home and I mean it, Avon.' He flicked the whip at the stolidly trotting horse and added, a trifle awkwardly: 'I hope you will be happy with us. It seems kind of odd, your father letting you go like that, his only child.' He was silent and Avon wondered if he was thinking of the daughter he had lost.

They had talked little on the drive out of town. The face on the poster and the words beneath it had driven all else from Avon's mind and she had been barely aware of the two business blocks, small park and scattered houses along a wide main street that made up the town of Miles City. The shock was still with her and she shivered and pulled her shawl around her shoulders. He had not looked a murderer, but perhaps such men did not carry their dreadful secret in their faces. Perhaps, in this raw rough country, murder was not uncommon. Men got

drunk and drew their guns too easily. Perhaps the
accused man had been in a fight and lost his temper. She
remembered his leap forward and the blow that had sent
the robber to the floor. With an effort she dragged her
thoughts away from him, the man whose face was there
for all to see, a wanted murderer, and turned to her
uncle, feeling her silence had been impolite.

'It is very good indeed of you and Aunt Rita to take
me,' she said quickly. 'I shall do all I can to please you
both and be of help. I am afraid my step-mother was not
willing to accept me. She has a daughter of her own, you
see.'

'Who isn't much of a beauty, I suppose,' her uncle said
dryly. 'It's hard on you, losing your mother and your
father marrying a woman with a cold nature.'

Avon was silent, her thoughts painful. She must forget
the past. She was entering a strange and somewhat
frightening life where she must learn new ways and be
grateful she had been given a home.

She wondered what her uncle meant by saying her
aunt might be 'stiff'. Had she not wanted to have her
husband's niece coming to live with them? Perhaps she
resented the idea of a stranger taking the place of the
daughter she had lost and who, had she lived, would now
be eighteen, the same age as Avon.

When her uncle asked about the hold-up she made no
mention of the man whose life she had saved and who
had treated her in so audacious and insulting a manner.
She felt nothing but angry contempt for his behaviour,
but something held her back from revealing his presence
on the train and his abrupt departure. He had taken a life
and must pay the penalty the law demanded. But she
would not help the law find him and—even though he
might deserve it—hang him.

They rattled through the small town of Sweetwater
where a barking dog was the only sign of life, and shop
signs creaked in the wind.

The farm lay in a shallow depression in the land. It was

dark, and when Ben got down to open the pasture gate, Avon could just make out a small, one-storey house with farm buildings around it. Light streamed from the open door as they drove up and a tall, spare woman wrapped in a shawl came onto the verandah steps and watched silently as Ben lifted Avon, now stiff with weariness from the long drive and longing for sleep, down from the buggy.

'Well, here she is, Rita,' the attempt at heartiness in her uncle's voice was a warning Avon was too tired to notice. 'Train got held up by road agents around Butte Bend, I guess there was valuables on board. Avon's had a poor welcome to the West.'

'I'm afraid I'm very late, Aunt Rita.' Avon roused herself to smile a little timidly at the forbidding, silent figure regarding her with deepset, expressionless eyes. 'I am sorry you have had to wait up.'

'I found work to do.' Her voice was harsh and unfriendly. 'You got those goods I wanted, Ben?'

'I got 'em.' Ben began to pull packages from the back of the buggy. 'You get Avon to bed, Rita, she's about dropping after all she's been through.'

Rita moved to one side of the doorway. 'Third door on the right.' She pointed down a passage. 'Don't keep the lamp on long, kerosene costs money.'

'Thank you.' Avon caught up her holdall and walked down the narrow passage with her head high. She would not let her aunt see the tears of disappointment and weariness gathering in her eyes. As she opened the door into a small room she heard her uncle say,

'Now Rita, that's no way to greet the girl, your niece.'

'*Your* niece, Ben Meredith! She's no niece of mine!'

Her aunt's voice came clearly and Avon knew she was meant to hear. She shut the door and set her bag on a chair, found a lamp and lit it and by its dim glow saw a small, bare room containing a brass bed, rough wooden table with jug and ewer, a framed text on one wall and two hooks on the back of the door. A rag rug was spread beside the bed and curtains made from flour sacks hung across the window.

She undressed, after unpacking a few things, and turned out the lamp. Before she got into bed she pulled aside the curtain and looked out into the silent, breathing darkness of the night, deeply aware of the vastness of this land that was to be her home, and the feeling of insignificance inspired by its tremendous horizons and great sweep of starry sky. She covered the window swiftly and retreated to her bed and sank into immediate, dreamless sleep.

A medley of sounds aroused her next morning. Hens clucking, a cow lowing, buckets clanking and voices outside her window.

A man asked: 'You taking the wagon in today, Texas?'

Another voice drawled: 'Nope, I plan to stay home and curl my hair. You can haul the goods to town and give the ladies a treat.'

She sprang out of bed and peeped out of the window. A stocky, bow-legged man with coarse white hair and nut-brown face was leaning against a fence, cutting a plug of tobacco. Near him, a young man was rubbing up a piece of harness. They must be her uncle's farm hands, men who helped him grow, harvest and market his produce.

She dressed swiftly, brushing her dark curls until they shone and trying them back with a pink ribbon. Her pink striped dress was perhaps a little too fashionable for farm life and she decided she must buy some material and make herself simpler clothes, and perhaps an apron. She noticed her aunt had worn one.

She stripped the bedclothes back to air the bed, wondering as she did so what the mattress was stuffed with which crackled so mysteriously, and then set out to find her way to the kitchen where she guessed she would find her aunt and uncle.

When she entered the room her uncle looked up from

the table where he sat, nodded, and went on with his meal. Her aunt was at the stove and did not turn as she said,

'You can sit down. Your breakfast's ready. Take your coffee.'

'Thank you, Aunt Rita.' Avon sat down and picked up the battered tin coffee pot her uncle pushed towards her. Her aunt placed a plate of eggs, ham and fried bread before her and returned to the black iron stove and Avon ate her breakfast in silence, wondering how she could break through her aunt's obvious antagonism. Perhaps she would never be able to, perhaps Rita would continue to resent having her husband's niece thrust upon her. The idea was not a happy one and she was glad when the white-haired man she had seen from her window entered and spoke to her uncle.

'Wagon's loaded, Ben, Curly's taking it in today. Should git a decent price for them chickens, Rita's sure fed 'em plump and pretty.' His eyes, dark and very bright despite his age, went to Avon and he bobbed his head.

'My niece, Avon,' Ben nodded towards her. 'She got held up when the Blackface gang looted her train.'

'I heard something of it,' the man said. 'Now that ain't in my opinion at all a purty way to welcome a young lady to the state of Montana.' He grinned at Avon, showing strong, tobacco-stained teeth. 'Name's Texas, Ma'am, and I'm sure glad to see you looking so perky after your brush with them road agents.'

'Best see Curly gets them crates packed tight,' Rita said sharply, 'he dropped one off last time. Your food'll be ready by the time you're back.'

'Can't I help you wash the dishes, Aunt Rita?' Avon asked, rising. 'Or is there anything else you would like me to do?'

'I've done all the work around here for thirty years, I guess I don't need help.'

Ben got to his feet. 'Now Rita, Avon's here and ready

to work and make herself useful. She's feeling strange and a bit lonely, missing her old home and friends.'

Rita swung around, a bright spot of colour in each cheek.

'And who asked her to leave her home and friends?'

'Now you know right well how it was,' Ben's voice was suddenly stern. 'Her father married a woman that didn't want her—and it seems *he* didn't want her either.' He watched his wife's lips tighten into a thin line. 'Don't say it, Rita, or maybe you'll regret it. Avon is my blood kin, and yours by marriage, and she's welcome in our home. She'll help with the work once she's got the hang of it.' He turned abruptly. 'I'm working on the north field today.'

Avon followed him out of the kitchen. At the door she caught up with him and said, a little breathlessly,

'I—I haven't yet truly thanked you, Uncle Ben, for giving me a home, but I *am* grateful, to you and Aunt Rita, and I will try my best to please you both.'

He nodded without looking at her and crossed the wide verandah that shaded the front of the house from the brilliant sunlight and disappeared into one of the barns.

Avon returned slowly to the kitchen where she found the man called Texas eating bacon and beans and drinking coffee from a tin mug. There was no sign of Rita. The man nodded affably and indicated the coffee pot.

'Made fresh and mighty good. Help yourself, Ma'am. Good coffee puts heart into you.'

So he knew she needed heartening. She sat down and reached for the pot, taken with a sudden liking for this tough, mild-spoken little man whose brown face was seamed with a hundred lines and whose dark eyes belied his drawl and lazy manner.

'You work for my uncle, don't you, Mr Texas?'

'You'll pardon me, Ma'am, but it don't seem natural to hear my name all spraddled out with a fancy handle. Just Texas does me fine.'

Avon laughed and her spirits rose a little. 'Very well,

Texas. But why am I "Ma'am"? I am not married.'

'Why I reckon all ladies out West is designated as Ma'am,' Texas told her, his face serious but with a twinkle in his eyes, 'us being a mighty respectful sex. But you being from England where I've heard folks don't speak 'less they've been interjooced, I'll say "Miss Meredith".'

'You will do no such thing, Texas,' Avon declared, leaning her elbows on the table, 'please call me Avon.'

He nodded, looking pleased. 'That's a right purty name, Avon.'

'It is the name of a river in the county where my mother was born.'

'Ben told me you lost your mother a while ago.'

'Yes. I—I still miss her. My father married again and my step-mother did not wish me to live with them.' She straightened her back, her head high and her eyes very bright as she looked at him. 'So you see, I had no home, until Uncle Ben agreed to give me one.'

She wondered why she was telling him this, a hired hand on her uncle's farm. Was it because he was the first person in whom she felt a warmth and a friendly interest in her?

'That sure was a hard deal,' he said soberly, pouring himself out more coffee. 'But Ben's a good man, he'll look after you. You won't mebbe find things go easy at first.' She guessed his meaning and her eyes dropped to her hands clasped in her lap. 'But don't let it rile you. Some folks won't let a wound heal. Farming's a hard life for womenfolk and there's some as grows bitter on it. Act like you don't notice nothing, Avon. That's my advice.'

'Thank you, Texas,' she whispered.

A sharp voice broke in, 'Are you going to spend the morning swilling coffee 'stead of getting on with your work, Texas?'

He finished his coffee and rose unhurriedly. 'I reckon you didn't ought to make such good coffee, Ma'am.'

Avon watched him amble out, feeling her only friend had left her.

'Since you're so anxious to get your hands dirty,' Rita said coldly, 'you can light into washing Texas's dishes— and don't forget to scrub up the table after, and wash out the dishcloths. I've to feed the chickens.'

Avon hastened to obey, glad to have something to do and to be alone while doing it. Her aunt had not wanted her and was set to continue resenting her presence in the house. She did not think her uncle resented her, undoubtedly she was making things difficult for him by upsetting his wife. She sighed as she filled the dishpan from the kettle and started washing the dishes. The soapy water splashed her dress and, looking around, she saw an apron hanging on a hook and removed it, tying it around her slender waist. She scrubbed the table as best she could, and carefully washed out the flour sacks used as dishcloths and went into the back yard to hang them on the line.

She went to her room and unpacked her clothes, but was puzzled where to put them as there were only two hooks on the door and a chair with a rush seat. She wondered if she could ask for a cupboard of some sort, or more hooks. But Rita would not listen and she did not like to worry her uncle about such a small matter.

While Rita was throwing corn to a swarm of hens and turkeys, Avon took the opportunity to explore the house. The plan of it was simple, a passage running through from front verandah to back porch, with rooms opening off it. Rita's and Ben's bedroom was on the right and on the left a room that must be the parlour. She opened the door and looked at the coloured prints, photographs and framed texts, the plush sofa and horse-hair chairs, crocheted mats under oil lamps with rose-patterned china globes and cushions stiff with woolwork and wondered if anyone ever sat there. The kitchen was at the back and her own small room opposite. Between her room and her aunt's was a storeroom, one corner of which Ben used as an office. The verandah ran the length of the house and had a homely air with its rocking chairs, hooked rug and pot plants.

Since Rita had now disappeared into the kitchen after a glance at Avon and a remark that she had best keep the apron until she bought some clothes that didn't look as if she was prinking up for a ball-dance, Avon decided to explore further and getting a shady hat, she set out down a path leading from the back porch down into a clump of cottonwoods and eventually, to her delight, to a charming little stream that chuckled lazily over stones and swirled around water weeds. It was refreshingly cool under the trees, listening to the water's song, and Avon lingered, sitting on the grass, her arms around her knees, letting her thoughts wander.

But as her thoughts turned to the hold-up on the train, some of her tranquillity was shattered. She could not help seeing again the tall, sunburned man sleeping opposite her, his hat over his face, the face she had seen yesterday at the depot. She saw a sudden blaze in his eyes as the robber approached her, and his move to prevent the man from touching her. When he said '—for a lady from England you moved pretty fast and furious —' he had smiled and she remembered because it so altered his face. And now she must see him for what he was, an outcast from society, a murderous criminal to be hunted down and . . . what? She shivered suddenly and got to her feet.

Back in the house, she seated herself on one of the rocking chairs and tried not to let a creeping dismay engulf her. As she rocked to and fro, her thoughts darkening, she heard a sound and looked up to see a rider approaching the house. As he stopped and swung down from his horse she recognised him as Haskin, the city sheriff and rose to meet him, grateful to be distracted from unhappy brooding on the future.

'Uncle Ben is in the north field,' she told him. 'I'll fetch my aunt.'

He came up the verandah steps and pulled off his wide hat, smiling at her.

'I guess maybe she'll be busy right now, Miss Meredith, we won't disturb her yet awhile. I came to see Ben, and also to ask how you were after your unfortunate experience on the train.'

'Oh, I am perfectly recovered,' she assured him. 'I shall have something to tell my friends when I write home. Won't you sit down?'

He sat down, after tossing his hat onto a peg, and stretched his legs out.

'It's sure time we got some rain,' he squinted up at the cloudless sky, 'seems we get too much of what we get. Crops will fail if this goes on. Last winter we had too much snow and frost and it finished many a man, cowman and farmer. They were hit real bad. I guess your uncle took quite a knock, losing his herd.'

'I didn't know he kept a herd.'

'Started a small one, reckoning to make butter and cheese and sell off calves, but he lost out.'

'Oh, poor Uncle Ben, he must have lost a lot of money.'

'Guess so. A small place like his don't make a fortune at the best of times.' He leant forward, his elbows on his knees, regarding her with a smile. 'And how are you making out, Miss Meredith? Seems kind of strange to you, maybe.'

'Yes, everything does,' she said frankly. 'I expect I'll soon learn.' She glanced down at her dress, she had removed the apron. 'I don't have the right clothes, I'm afraid. When Uncle Ben goes into Sweetwater next I must go with him and buy some dress cotton.'

'Seems a mighty pretty dress to me,' he remarked, leaning back. 'You'll maybe get what you want at Muller's store, he sells dress goods.' He got to his feet as Rita came onto the verandah. 'Morning, Ma'am. I was enquiring after your niece.'

'She's Ben's niece, not mine.' Rita's sharpness of tone

made the sheriff's thick eyebrows rise and he glanced at Avon before saying,

'That so? Ben's a lucky man. I'll ride out to Ben, I'm dropping a word with folk around these parts. There's a man we want that may be hiding out someplace south of the city.' He took his hat off the peg and turned to Avon. 'He's the man I was asking you about on the train. We've news he may be the man who called at a farm saying he'd had to shoot his horse after an accident. He bought a horse, a good one, and paid cash. It's my guess he lit out south.'

Rita's eyes widened. 'Is he named Ken Grant?' The sheriff nodded. 'He's wanted for a killing, ain't he?'

'Yep. Shot an unarmed man in a saloon brawl, a witness saw it. He bust out of jail and they lost him. But he once worked in these parts and knows the country and he might be making for the Indian Hills.'

'He could ride out there a twelvemonth and you'd not get him,' Rita remarked.

'The law has a long arm, Ma'am,' the sheriff said quietly. 'I'll be saying *adios*.'

Avon turned from watching him ride off, thinking how well he sat his big sorrel horse, and found Rita's eyes on her.

'Quite the lady, ain't you?' The lines on her thin face seemed to deepen. 'Setting on the porch, entertaining company—*gentlemen* company!'

'I was talking to him until you came, it seemed only polite.'

'Well, in this country it seems like a girl makes herself mighty cheap to be flirting with a man old enough to be her father!'

'I was *not* flirting!' Abruptly Avon was gripped with a fierce anger. She flung all her good resolutions to behave meekly and win Rita's approval to the wind as the words poured out. 'I have not behaved badly and you know it! You dislike me, you did not wish to take me in. You have been unkind, even rude, to me since I arrived! I was going to try and please you, to make you like, or at least, tolerate me, but now I do not care! You can hate me as much as you please! You will not force me to leave . . . that is what you are trying to do, isn't it?' She clenched her hands, her eyes blazing. 'Well you won't! Uncle Ben said this is my home—and I mean to stay!'

She finished, breathless and shaken by her passionate outburst. For a moment there was complete silence while she stood, awaiting Rita's wrath to fall upon her.

A peculiar sound came from her aunt, a cross between a snort and a sniff.

'Well, for lands sake, so you ain't filled with sawdust after all.' To Avon's astonishment she saw Rita's face had lost some of its grimness. 'You sure got a burr under your saddle! Here,' she pulled off her apron and tossed it to Avon, 'go set the table for dinner 'stead of trying to burn my skin with them eyes of yours. And holler to Texas you want eggs and a cabbage.'

As in a daze, Avon tied on the apron and entered the house. Was she mistaken, or *had* she seen a tiny flicker of amusement in Rita's sunken eyes?

CHAPTER
THREE

I N the days following her arrival at the farm, Avon
slowly got used to a life that was different in every
respect from the life she had known in England. It was a
simpler, rougher, harder life and there were times when
the longing for her own country and friends became
almost unbearable. But she hid her dismay and tried to
put away memories and learn to make the best of her
situation.

Her aunt remained cold and at times harsh in her
condemnation of the mistakes Avon made and what she
called her 'fancy-frilled airs'. But she had not actually
been rude since Avon's brief flare-up. She grudgingly
allowed Avon to help clean the house and feed the
chickens and make the butter which was sold in
Sweetwater along with chickens and ducks, vegetables
and melons. Sometimes Ben took a wagon load of
produce into Miles City and brought back supplies which
could not be bought in Sweetwater. The farm was a small
one, but the soil was rich and it was well watered and the
great ragged range to the west known as the Indian Hills
broke some of the winds that could scour the plains at
times.

Texas had worked for Ben for two years. No one knew
much about him. He had come up from the south with a
leg injury that barred him from ranch work and Ben had
hired him, thinking him a drifter who would soon move
off. But Texas stayed on. His placid acceptance of Rita's
acid treatment exasperated her but she knew it was not
easy to get farm help in a ranching country and she had
to admit Texas's drawl and lazy movement did not

prevent his being a very handy man to have around the farm.

Some days after she arrived Avon found a rack with six pegs nailed up on her wall. Later on, a neatly-made wooden chest appeared in which she could keep her clothes. She guessed from whom they had come even before she heard Ben demanding of Rita what in thunder Texas was doing in the barn sawing and hammering when the back fence needed rewiring.

When she tried to thank him, Texas became highly embarrassed. His weather-beaten face turned a dusky purple and he shuffled his feet, muttering something about a room not being set up right for a young lady.

'It was very kind of you, Texas,' she told him. 'My dresses were getting very creased hanging over a chair.'

'Nothing to thank me for,' he said hurriedly, backing out of the kitchen, 'carpentry's a kind of hobby with me, I guess.'

Although she had not heard his name mentioned again, Avon could not banish the memory of Ken Grant from her mind. She supposed it was because of her first, startling introduction to her new life in which he had taken part, that his face with its ice-blue eyes stayed so clearly in her thoughts. She felt deep abhorrence for him. That he had insulted her was nothing compared with his crime, the killing of an unarmed man in a brawl. Those chill blue eyes were the eyes of a killer. He was ruthless, cunning, an outlaw to be hunted down by the law.

She went with Texas on one of his trips into Sweetwater and visited Muller's Fashion Emporium, a ramshackle building with a high false front and faded awnings, and bought materials to make herself some simple gowns and three aprons. Her father had given her money and promised her a tiny income so she would not become a burden on her uncle.

Rita eyed the frills on the aprons, and the pretty

buttons—taken from one of the too-smart London dresses—that decorated the blue checked alpaca made for Sunday best, but forbore to comment. Her own clothes were drab and ill-fitting and made for hard wear with no concession to fashion. She wore men's boots and screwed her still plentiful hair into a bun at the top of her head. From Texas Avon learned that her aunt was the daughter of a Dakota rancher and could still 'handle a balky yearling if she's a mind to'.

The other farm hand was Curly, a lanky youth who had left home at fifteen and drifted from job to job with no particular aim in life and who, as soon as he saw Avon, promptly fell in love with her, a condition which turned his face scarlet whenever she met him and caused Ben to threaten to fire him if he didn't quit behaving like a lovesick burro.

One morning Rita remarked at breakfast: 'Obie Skellar was by yesterday and says they're having a get-together for Pheelie's eighteenth birthday. Seems he thinks I'll go along, but I told him I'd no time to waste getting dressed up and mixing social with neighbours.'

Ben looked up from his beans and bacon. 'I'd say you should go. The Skellars are our nearest neighbours, and their two girls would be company for Avon. If it's to be a party, she'll meet people.'

'She don't have any more time to waste than I do,' Rita said firmly. 'The Skellars are just squirrel-curious to see her.'

'I say you'd best take her,' Ben said. 'You liked a party yourself when you were a girl. I met you at one.'

Rita sniffed and began to collect the dishes. 'If it's husband-chasing you're at, Ben, Avon won't meet anyone she'd take a fancy to, not with her fancy ideas. She's been used to mixing with lords and ladies and high-tone folk.'

Ben pushed his empty plate aside and rose. 'You take her, Rita. Tex'll give the buggy a polish.'

'Texas has better things to do.'

'I said you'll take her to the Skellars.' There was no mistaking the authority in Ben's voice and Avon saw Rita's lips tighten before she turned to the sink.

The idea of meeting neighbours and some young people raised Avon's spirits and she was singing as she carried corn out to the fowls. Texas came out of the barn holding a saddle and harness and grinned at her.

'Ain't heard a prettier bird singing in these parts ever,' he observed, pausing beside her.

'Aunt Rita is taking me to a birthday party with some family called Skellar,' she told him gaily.

'Reckon she didn't do it willing,' Texas said shrewdly. 'Rita don't have much truck with her neighbours.'

'What sort of people are the Skellars?' she asked, resting the bowl on one hip.

Texas scratched his leathery cheek reflectively, 'Wal, Obadiah Skellar ain't done bad with his ranch, it's nothing fancy but he keeps good breeds and gets good prices for 'em.'

'And his wife?'

Texas squinted up at the sky. 'Me, I don't never say nothing derogatory 'bout a woman. Mrs Mame Skellar dresses smart, and keeps a cook and goes to church regular.'

'That doesn't really tell me much,' Avon complained. 'What is the family?'

'Two girls and a young son. Miss Ophelia—'

'Is she Pheelie?'

'Yep. She's a right purty girl and knows it. She's turned a heap of young fellows loco about her. Her sister Daisy is no beauty but she's good-hearted. I guess you'll take to Daisy.' He shifted the saddle under his arm. 'Can you ride, Avon?'

'Yes, I had lessons in England.'

'You'd best practise up a bit, riding's important out West. Ben's got a young filly that's lady-broke. I'll saddle her up and you can take her nice and gentle around the fields till you both get acquainted.'

The idea delighted Avon. Ben gave his consent and Rita appeared to approve. Suddenly Avon remembered something.

'Well, what's eating you?' Rita demanded on seeing her face fall.

'I didn't bring my riding habit with me and my dresses are not suitable for riding, I'm afraid.'

Rita said nothing, but later in the day she came into Avon's room and thrust a bundle into her arms, saying briefly,

'Reckon these'll fit. A divided skirt's safer than petticoats. You can have 'em.'

She walked out before Avon could thank her. The slit skirt, checked cotton blouse and riding boots must have belonged to Minna, the daughter who died, and fitted well. When Avon tried to thank her aunt she was told to quit gabbing and get on shelling beans.

The Skellar party was on a Saturday. Texas had smartened up the buggy with polish and a bit of paint. When Avon appeared, entrancingly pretty in rose muslin and a shady hat with rose ribbons, Texas shifted his wad of tobacco to the other cheek and wagged his head.

'I reckon Pheelie Skellar won't be riding so tail-high when she gets a look at you, Avon. She's been the purtiest gal in the district—till now.'

Avon laughed and returned to the house to see if her aunt was ready. She found Rita tying a clean apron around her waist. Her dress was her everyday brown cotton and her expression was such that Avon hesitated a moment before saying,

'I think . . . I'm sure you'd look smarter without an apron, Aunt Rita.'

Rita's dark eyes snapped as she faced Avon. 'I ain't elegant enough, I suppose, to be seen with you! Well, I've got a *smart* dress and I ain't putting it on for a Skellar shindig! This dress is clean, that's good enough.'

She stared as she saw Avon opening the cupboard.

'Why, Aunt Rita, this is charming.' Avon pulled out a _

red foulard gown with black braiding. 'The colour will suit you so well.'

'You put it right back!'

Avon met her aunt's angry eyes squarely. 'I think you should wear it. People might think Uncle Ben cannot afford to give you nice dresses.'

'I take no note of what people choose to say.'

'Well I do—and I expect Uncle Ben does too. And I'm pretty sure you do too, Aunt Rita, in your heart.'

For a second Avon thought Rita would snatch the dress from her. Then a curious expression crossed her thin, bitter face and she turned away, saying over her shoulder,

'Lay it on the bed and get out.'

Avon was in the buggy when Rita came out wearing the red foulard. She had arranged her hair in a plait around her head and the difference in her appearance was startling. There was a becoming flush on her cheeks which were usually so sallow, and she shot a fiery glance at Texas when he bowed with elaborate courtesy before helping her into the buggy and handing her the reins.

'You get them ducks killed and plucked 'fore I get back,' she snapped, 'and keep away from that bottle of red-eye you got hid in the bunkhouse.' She whipped up the horse to a smart pace, her head high and her mouth tight.

The Skellars' ranch lay some three miles from Ben's farm. The house was the usual long, rambling building with a wide verandah on which a group of people were collected. A small, plump woman in a tight purple gown came forward as Rita and Avon came up the steps. Her fair hair was arranged with elaborate care and her array of bracelets jangled as she shook hands.

'Well, I certainly am pleased to see you, Rita. It ain't often we meet now.' She looked at Avon. 'And this is Ben's niece I guess. My, the girls will be just so pleased to have a new friend. Pheelie! Daisy! Come right over and greet your new neighbour, Avon Meredith from England.'

Avon looked at the girls who came forward with interest. Pheelie, the elder, was indeed a beauty with huge, light blue eyes and golden curls and an assured manner. Her sister was a slender girl with dull brown hair and small, undistinguished features except for rather lovely soft brown eyes. Both girls were elaborately dressed and Mrs Skellar's pride in her daughters was evident in the fondly admiring look she bent upon them as she said,

'Now you girls take Miss Meredith around and see she gets to meet folk, this is her first chance to get acquainted with neighbours.'

'I'm really pleased to know you, Miss Meredith,' Pheelie murmured languidly. 'I guess you find things different from England? When I get back from visiting in Boston, I certainly do miss town ways and society.'

She turned away to speak to someone. Suddenly a hand touched Avon's arm and Daisy said gently,

'Please come with me, Miss Meredith. I'd like you to meet Becky Svenson, and Kate Jonson and the McCormack girls.'

Avon shook hands with the group of girls who greeted her gaily, asking questions about England, London, the Queen and the latest fashions, and she began to feel at home. Daisy stayed beside her and as they moved into the house, she said suddenly,

'There's Frank Carline, he owns the Two-Bar ranch. He's English too.'

Avon turned her head and saw a slim young man in a grey suit talking to Pheelie. As if he sensed her gaze, he turned and she felt a stir of interest as she met his dark eyes. He had been laughing at something Pheelie said, but as his eyes met Avon's the laugh died out of them and a startled, suddenly intent look took its place. Avon's fingers tightened on the little reticule she carried, aware of a tiny quickening in her blood. He was extraordinarily handsome, his well-cut features and air of authority making him stand out among the coarser, rougher men around him. For a moment his eyes held hers, then she turned to Daisy and asked, a little breathlessly,

'You say he is English?'

'Yes. He came out West four years ago and has learned the ranching business mighty quick, they say. The Two-Bar spread is one of the best in these parts, and his house is really fine. I'll call him over.'

But as she spoke, a voice said beside her: 'Won't you introduce me, Daisy? I believe your friend has recently come out from England.'

'Why yes. Meet Frank Carline, Miss Meredith. She's niece to Ben Meredith, Frank. I guess you two will find a heap to talk about.'

'I shall be delighted, if Miss Meredith can spare me the time.' He smiled and again Avon's interest was aroused. He was attractive, perhaps the most attractive man she had met. His fine dark eyes were warmly friendly—and unmistakably admiring as he led her across the room to a table loaded with food.

After he had provided her with a plate of chicken salad and a glass of iced lemonade, he found a corner of the verandah where they were away from the crowd and asked her how she liked Western life, and she found herself talking freely of the strangeness of much of her life and her hope that she would soon find it less strange.

'It took me some time to get accustomed to living out here,' he said.

'What made you come?'

He shrugged. 'I got tired of the political life my father wished me to follow, so I threw it up and decided to come to America and take on ranching. I've always liked a country life and Montana is a fine state.' He smiled. 'I wasn't popular at first, of course. Folk called me a greenhorn and waited for me to fail.'

'But you didn't,' she said quickly.

'No, I didn't.' He looked out across the wide stretch of grassland to the line of distant hills. 'This country had tremendous possibilities. It is new and largely undiscovered land and there is room for a man to feel free to live as he wishes.'

'But isn't ranching hard work? And isn't the climate sometimes cruel?' she asked.

'That is true, Miss Meredith. We had a winter recently that took a sad toll of many herds. I was lucky, but many cowmen got it badly.'

'I think yours is a fine achievement,' Avon said, and said it with sincerity. She knew few young men at home who would have given up a comfortable life in England for the hard and rough life men lived in the American West. 'You must have worked hard to make such a success possible.'

He leant forward, his face eager. 'Do you truly mean that? Then I appreciate it more than I can tell you, Miss Meredith. If I thought—'

'Frank Carline, I've been . . . Mama has been looking all over for you!' Pheelie Skellar stood before them and as Frank rose, her eyes, distinctly frosty, flicked over Avon. 'She wants you to talk to Pa about the last rustlers' raid on the Barlow herd. Pa gets kind of restless at parties,' she condescended to explain to Avon, ' 'less he can talk cow-talk with someone.'

She laid her hand on Frank's arm as she drew him away, smiling at him. 'Excuse us, Miss Meredith.'

Avon bowed politely. She had not missed the irritation that had flashed across Frank Carline's handsome face, or the chill in Pheelie's eyes when she had spied them together. So the local beauty considered Frank her property. Avon's eyes followed the pair thoughtfully as she finished her plate of food and she wondered what Frank's feelings were about the pretty Miss Skellar. Was he attracted to her, as she obviously was to him? Perhaps they were engaged, or about to be. Pheelie's manner was possessive and Frank, despite his momentary annoyance, had obeyed her and gone into the house.

A man's voice aroused her from her thoughts.

'I was thinking maybe I would see you here, Miss Meredith. May I sit by you?'

She looked up to see Sheriff Haskin standing over her, looking very large and forceful. She smiled up at him as she indicated the chair beside her.

'Please do, I seem to have lost my partner.'

He grinned as he seated himself beside her. 'Miss Pheelie has high-handed ways with menfolk.'

'Why not? It is her birthday. Are you here socially or on duty?' She laced her fingers together and regarded him demurely. 'Do you suspect someone may steal Mrs Skellar's teaspoons— or are you trailing the men who raided the Barlow herd?'

'So you've heard about the rustlers' latest haul?'

Her eyes widened. 'Their latest? Have there been other raids?'

The sheriff's face was suddenly grim. 'Too many for my liking. Cattle are being rustled in a mighty clever way and no sign of who's boss of the gang who are operating the stealing. There are large spreads around these parts and straying cattle can be hived off, hidden and re-branded before being trailed to a railroad depot and shipped east.'

'And you have no idea who this gang is?'

He shrugged his heavy shoulders. 'There's some say it's another activity of the Blackface gang, and maybe it is. It's known they've held up banks as well as trains, so maybe rustling is another hobby of theirs.'

'And you are down here to investigate?' Avon asked with interest.

'Could be.' He grinned at her. 'And it could be I'm interested in a certain gent that was on your train and who vamoosed somewhere along the line and got himself a horse and ain't been met since.'

Avon looked at him quickly. 'You mean the man they call Ken Grant who—'

'Who's wanted for a cowardly murder down in Laramie and who I suspicion is hiding out someplace around these parts.'

'Has he been seen by anyone?'

'Well, a lonesome horseman was seen a couple of times high on a ridge of the Indian Hills who seemed kind of shy of meeting anyone. It seems likely it might be Grant prospecting for a hide-out . . . or keeping a watch for any curious folk on the trail of rustlers.'

Something cold touched Avon for a second. She said, 'You mean—Ken Grant might be connected with stealing cattle?'

'A man don't often stop at one crime, Miss Meredith. Grant could have operated from the south and come up to take charge of his gang—or hide from the law. A sky rider sure has his reasons, and they ain't often good ones.'

'But you don't know for certain Ken Grant is the—what did you call him?—the sky rider, do you, Sheriff?'

'No,' he got up, hooking his thumbs in his belt. 'I don't know, Miss Meredith, but I darn well mean to find out.'

She watched him walk away, a strong, determined man and highly efficient officer of the law. A man who would ruthlessly hunt down those men who committed crimes and fled from the consequences to hole up in the secret hide-outs of the outlaws who infested the country. He had left the city to pursue the trail of one such outlaw, a man whose life she had saved and who had kissed her as she had never been kissed before. Had Grant come to this part of the state because he would know where to hide, or to pursue his rustling of cattle? If he *was* a cattle thief as well as murderer.

As she sat looking unseeingly across sunlit pastures she had a sudden mental vision of a lone horseman silhouetted against an evening sky and she shivered. He would not escape the law. He would be hunted like a wild and dangerous animal. Every man's hand would be against him, every eye searching the jagged heights of the Indian Hills, seeking that solitary figure, the sky rider!

CHAPTER
FOUR

AFTER the Skellars' party Avon's life became more social. Daisy rode over sometimes to see her as did some of the girls she had met. They inspected her clothes, told her the latest gossip and giggled over their men friends' attentions and behaved, Rita remarked acidly, like a bunch of newly hatched chicks that didn't know nothing but how to cheep. But she let Avon provide coffee for the afternoon gatherings on the porch.

Pheelie Skellar did not come. Avon met her on the dusty sidewalk in Sweetwater one morning when Texas had taken her in in the wagon, and the lovely Miss Skellar bestowed a cool bow on her and pointedly ignored Texas's swept-off hat.

'Guess she don't know I'm here,' he remarked as Pheelie rustled away, holding her skirts high to avoid the dust, 'me not being the handsome owner of the best ranching outfit around here.'

'You mean Frank Carline?'

'So you've met up with him? You ain't aiming to set your rope on him, Avon?'

'Of course not. Anyway,' she glanced after Pheelie's disappearing figure, 'I think there is another who is—is setting her rope on him.'

'Guess you must of met him at the Skellars' bun wrassle. Handsome young fellow, ain't he?'

'He is very good-looking,' she agreed. 'I found him pleasant to talk to.'

'Sure you would, seeing you and him come from the same country.'

'I admire him for the success he has made out here,'

she said, and had a sudden memory of the eager look in
Frank Carline's eyes when she had told him so.

'Yep, he learned fast,' Texas agreed. 'You got much
buying to do now?'

'I want some shoe polish for Aunt Rita, and a few
things for myself.'

Texas hitched up his belt. 'First time I've knowed Rita
think of polishing her boots.'

'She hasn't,' Avon told him, 'but I have. I'm hoping
she will buy herself some smarter footwear one day.'

'Don't wear yourself out hoping. I've to deliver this
load, get grain feed and a sack of flour.'

'I've promised to call on Kate Jonson at her home, will
you call for me there?'

He nodded. 'Mrs Jonson runs a rooming house in
Cross Street, next the church. I'll be along 'bout near
noon.'

Kate Jonson was a big, healthy girl who had taken an
immediate fancy to Avon. She worked in her mother's
boarding house and never complained of a life that was
hard and allowed little time for fun or freedom. Her
father was dead and Mrs Jonson had turned their home
into a rooming house where she took in the school
teacher, visiting ranchers and the preacher when he
made his visits to hold services in the little red-brick
church. There was little money to spare in the Jonson
household and Avon admired and liked the girl who
made a cheerful thing out of a hard life.

Kate was shaking mats out of a window when Avon
arrived.

She called out: 'Come right in, Avon, Ma's got coffee
on the stove and she's made hot biscuits, figuring you'd
eaten early.'

Avon went into the kitchen where Kate joined her.
The hot flaky scones—which Avon had learned to call
biscuits—were dripping with butter and very welcome
after the drive into town.

'I've got a real nice bit of news for you,' Kate declared,

spooning grape jelly onto her biscuit. 'Folk are getting up a picnic out to the Indian Hills. The new teacher is letting the older kids out for the day and there's to be five wagonloads of us. Ma's making cakes and some of the girls will be setting to baking cookies. I guess everyone's fixing something. Will your aunt let you bake something, Avon?'

'I'm not even sure she will let me go,' Avon said ruefully. 'She won't come herself, I am certain; she doesn't care for social events. She may not like to have me away for a whole day, it will mean more work for her and—'

'Well, for mercy's sake, don't she want you to have some fun?' Kate demanded indignantly. 'There's plenty of work right here, but Ma don't expect me to spend every minute of my life at it. You ask her real nice and gentle, Avon, or . . .' she looked thoughtful ' . . . or maybe you'd best ask your uncle, you're sure pretty enough to get round him if you try.'

Avon laughed. 'I don't think Uncle Ben notices what I look like. He is a rather . . . rather reserved man and never says much. I really don't know him very well.'

Kate nodded. 'Most folks say the same. Ben Meredith sure had bad luck losing out on ranching and then losing Minna.'

'Did you know her?'

'Oh sure. We 'tended school together and she was a nice kid, but a mite quiet, like her pa. She got pneumonia one winter and died. Folks say your aunt ain't been the same woman since.'

'It must have been a great sorrow to her.'

'We was all wondering how she'd take having Ben's niece come to live with them,' Kate said frankly. 'Rita Meredith ain't a woman to change her ways. Maybe you recall Minna to her at times.'

Avon was silent. This was something she had wondered about herself.

On the way home Avon told Texas about the proposed picnic to the Indian Hills.

'You'll like that, Avon. Young folks get a heap of fun from a day's picnic in them hills, there's some watered valleys that'll be cool and nice for parties.'

'If Aunt Rita will let me go.'

Texas leaned over the wagon side to squirt out a stream of tobacco juice before saying.

'She'll maybe act kind of mean at first, but she'll unhitch your rope later, I reckon.'

'Well, I hope so,' Avon sighed. 'I would love to spend a day in the hills with the girls.'

'Won't only be females,' Texas snorted, jerking the reins. 'Ain't a young fellow in fifty miles won't try to slip his rope to join in. Picnics is like honey to 'em.'

'I'll be glad to meet them,' Avon declared gaily.

'Nothing like how glad they'll be when they set eyes on you,' Texas warned. 'You'd best keep a gun handy to fight 'em off.'

Avon chuckled. 'I'm afraid I haven't got a gun. Perhaps I could borrow yours?'

'I don't tote a gun,' he told her. 'Never trusted the pesky things, they goes off too sudden and dangerous for me.'

'I thought every man carried—I mean toted—a gun out West.'

'You got a heap to learn about the West, I reckon.'

Avon's thoughts kept returning to the picnic all the rest of the day. Rita had taken her to the Skellars' party but only because Ben had insisted. Would it be best, Avon wondered as she ironed her and her aunt's aprons on the kitchen table, to approach her uncle first? But that might make Rita angry and even if Ben said she could go, it would do nothing to improve the situation between herself and her aunt. Perhaps she had better say nothing; and yet the picture of wagons packed with lively young boys and girls making for the hills she had so often looked at, hills that were sometimes so near and sometimes so far off, persisted and made her restless and depressed.

Then at supper, her uncle spoke of it.

'I had a word with Obie Skellar and he tells me there's a town picnic being got up next week. They'll hold it in the Indian Hills. His girls are all set to go.'

'To show off the fancy clothes Mame Skellar buys for 'em every time she sets eyes on a fashion paper,' Rita said. 'Some folks have nothing better to do than piroot-ing around eating food in the open and acting real silly.'

Avon's heart sank and she pushed away her plate of chicken and corn.'

Rita went on: 'I don't hold with such foolishness . . . What's wrong with your supper, Avon?'

'I'm not very hungry, Aunt Rita.'

Ben reached for the pitcher of milk. 'I told Obie his wagon can call for Avon. His girls plan to start early.'

Avon looked up, her face flushed and a sparkle in her grey eyes.

'I can go?'

'I suppose so, since your uncle is set on spoiling you sick,' Rita snapped. 'You can finish your supper now your appetite's come back.'

Daisy came over next day to discuss plans. 'Pa's letting us have the big wagon and we're to start off around seven, Avon. It's over three hours drive to the foothills and we want to find shade and water. We're taking Kate and two other girls and the Hobson boys and the preacher. Ma don't care for picnics.'

'What about your brother?' Avon remembered the small, red-headed boy she had seen riding around the ranch.

'Oh, Ted'll be along, he'll likely ride with the men. Frank Carline and some of his hands will be riding with us, we'll be a fine big party.'

All that week Avon's thought lingered on the picnic in the hills. If the memory of Frank Carline's dark eyes obtruded, she told herself it was natural she would wish to see him again, a countryman of hers in a land where she was a stranger.

Rita said no more about the outing, but her manner was colder towards Avon and she did not speak to her often.

When the day came, Avon decided to wear her best dress, the blue check alpaca. As she pinned her mother's little watch on the bodice of her dress she remembered how near she had once come to losing it to the man with the ugly birthmark and the scene in the railway car came back to her with curious force. The man who had prevented it, the man who had slipped from the train, bought himself a horse and disappeared, according to Sheriff Haskin was probably hiding out in the same hills she was to visit that day, skulking in some canyon or cave.

Even if he were not a rustler, he would probably have friends who were. Criminals stick together and he might now be sharing the robbers' hold-out, the hidden place where cattle were driven to have old brands obliterated and new brands burned on, the place the sheriff was seeking.

She had no knowledge how far the hills stretched or how they lay, but Texas had told her they were 'like a piece of crumpled paper', with narrow gorges formed by rivers cutting through the soft rock of an arid region, slopes seamed with gullies, side canyons thick with scrub and benchlands gnashed with coulees.

They were not exceptionally high mountains but appeared so because they rose so abruptly from the plains.

'Reckon they're badlands,' Texas had said. 'Riding there ain't no amusement for sure, a man could lose himself mighty quick among all them ravines and ridges.'

Avon was on the verandah when the Skellar wagon rolled up. Her cheeks were softly flushed and her grey eyes, under their slender, arched brows, were alight with excitement and joyful anticipation. Her gown was made in simple style and had nothing of the fussy elegance of Pheelie's yellow cambric dress with its modish draped skirt and lacy bodice, but it was very much more appropriate to a picnic, and her wide hat made it unnecessary for her to carry a parasol such as Pheelie was twirling provocatively in the front seat of the wagon as she looked at Frank Carline riding beside her.

Frank looked well on a horse. He swept off his hat when he saw Avon and dismounted to help her up into the wagon.

'I trust we are not too early for you, Miss Meredith?'

She assured him he was not. He remounted and was talking to some friends when Avon saw her aunt come out onto the verandah holding a basket. She peered around and, seeing Avon, came up to her side of the wagon.

'I made a burnt-sugar cake for your uncle,' she said shortly. There was a tight look about her mouth that made Avon draw back instinctively. 'It's his favourite and I sure didn't mean to waste it on a lot of young folk that'd be better employed doing their proper work, but Ben, he says I'm to give it.'

Something rose in Avon's throat, choking her. Everyone else's family had baked and prepared food for the picnic except Rita. The cake had not been meant for her, it was her uncle's and he had made Rita offer it.

As the driver gathered up the reins of the two-horse team, Avon looked directly into Rita's dark eyes and said coolly,

'Thank you, but I don't want it. Daisy says there is enough for everyone.'

Rita stepped back quickly. Red burned in her thin cheeks for a moment, then receded, leaving her white. The wagon and its laughing load set off down the track leading to the main road. Something made Avon turn her head. Rita was standing on the verandah steps, holding the basket and staring after them. There was a curious rigidity in her spare figure and Avon had a twinge of conscience. But it was her aunt's fault, she told herself. An offering so ungraciously made deserved rejection. She turned to Kate Jonson who was chatting happily about the day's weather prospects.

'Guess it's set for a fine day. That's a mighty pretty dress you're wearing, Avon. My! You've got an elegant curvy figure.' She sighed gustily. 'Me, I've got too much in the wrong places.'

Pheelie's voice floated back to them. 'Now Frank Carline, you've no right to say such things! Pa says a grizzly won't attack 'less you go for him. You're just trying to scare me and you should be real ashamed of yourself!'

'I am,' Frank agreed. 'I don't deserve the honour of riding beside you any longer. I'll drop back and repent me of my sins.'

He reined in his horse and waited until he was along-side Avon before riding on. His dark eyes met hers and once more she felt a little shock of excitement tingle through her.

'I hope you will enjoy your first Western-style picnic, Miss Meredith,' he said.

'Oh, I know I will,' she assured him fervently. 'I've often looked at the Indian Hills and longed to visit them, they have an odd fascination for me.'

Ted Skellar brought his picnic pony up to trot beside Frank.

'I guess those hills are pretty useful if a badman wants to hide out from the law,' he said with relish. 'Maybe we'll come across some! Pa says a man could hide for half his lifetime in the ravines and caves.'

'Do you want to meet a badman, Ted?' Avon asked, smiling down at the red-headed, freckled boy. 'If you did meet one, what would you do?'

'Track him to where he's at,' Ted said promptly, 'and tell the sheriff. Maybe I'd find stolen cattle, and money looted from the train hold-ups and banks—'

'And maybe get yourself shot in the process,' Frank said. 'Doug Haskin has this idea there's a wanted man hiding in the hills.'

'You mean Ken Grant?' Avon asked quickly.

'Yes, but Haskin is wrong, he can stop looking. Grant will be heading west by now, he'll make for the Rockies.'

'Say, that's too bad,' Ted looked disappointed. 'If I'd cotched him I'd have gotten the reward.'

'Then he isn't this sky rider who's been seen?' Avon said.

'He may have been, but it's my guess he's out west by now.'

'Sheriff Haskin told me he—Ken Grant—was on my train when I was coming to Miles City.'

'Why gee, Miss Meredith,' Ted's freckled face expressed deep disgust, 'You could have held him and handed him over and got the reward.'

'Unfortunately Miss Meredith doesn't carry a gun,' Frank told him, smiling, 'and I don't suppose she even saw him, much less knew who he was.'

'Frank,' Pheelie's voice rang out. 'The other wagons are coming up, ride over and tell them the way we're taking.'

Frank did not appear to hear her. He rode a little closer to the wagon and held Avon in conversation, asking questions about the country he had not seen for so long, and, when she asked, telling her of the Two-Bar ranch he owned.

'I would be greatly honoured if you and your aunt and uncle would come out on a visit,' he said. 'It is not so far, and if Mr Meredith could take a Sunday off and bring you . . . Do you think he would, Miss Meredith?'

'Oh, I hope he will!' Avon said impulsively. She felt the colour rise in her cheeks and added hastily: 'I—I mean, I haven't yet seen a big ranch. I would be most interested.' She dropped her eyes under his steady gaze and asked: 'Have you lost any cattle to rustlers, Mr Carline?'

'By heaven's mercy, no,' he replied, 'but my turn may come.'

'Do they hide the stolen cattle in the hills?'

He shook his head. 'I'm certain they don't. The cattle are taken at night from outlying herds so they will not be missed for some days and by that time they are on their way to be shipped, bearing a faked brand.'

'How do they fake a brand?' she asked curiously.

'Burn out the old one and burn on a new one over a wet blanket so it will look old,' he told her. 'Miss Meredith—'

A burst of shouting drowned what he intended to say. Four wagons loaded with school children and two with townsfolk had driven up with riders on either side. Greetings were exchanged and the teacher endeavoured to restrain his tribe of excited youngsters. Avon watched the scene with interest and amusement. She was too occupied to notice the many curious glances directed at her or the frank admiration in most of the young men's eyes. She saw Pheelie waving her parasol at Frank who rode up to her.

At last the wagon train set off and people settled down for the drive in the hot sunlight. The wagons' canvas tops kept off the direct rays of the scorching sun, but the heat became uncomfortable after a time and Avon was relieved as she watched the hills slowly draw nearer with their promise of cool shade from trees. Dust rose, making her throat dry, but despite her discomfort she was enthralled by all she saw, the flat grasslands and the occasional strange shape of a butte rising abruptly, its weird formation sculptured by long erosion. Curlews sailed low over the grass, their long bills stretched out as they gave their harsh cry. Suddenly her eye caught sight of a group of horsemen and she cried,

'Oh! Indians!'

'Haven't you seen them before?' Frank had ridden up beside her again. 'They are Sioux and live mostly on the plains, but a few have taken to the hills. They need not frighten you, they're friendly.'

'If they ever cotched you and behaved bad, you just make out like you're crazy,' Ted told her. 'Sioux won't never touch no one who's loco 'cause they think they're full of bad spirits.'

'Thank you, Ted,' she said gravely, 'I'll take care to remember that.'

The wagons rumbled over the rough track, sometimes dipping down to cross a dry river bed and often winding between the low hills scattered over the approach to the foothills. Pink, yellow and blue wildflowers grew on hill slopes and in spite of the dust and heat, Avon felt a growing attachment to the wild and beautiful country that was to be her home. There was a feeling of grandeur in it, of great spaces untouched by man, of freedom and eternal, silent loveliness.

Impulsively she turned to Frank. 'I don't wonder you chose to stay here, it is magnificent!'

'You feel it too?' he said quickly. 'I've hoped you would, Miss Meredith . . . Avon.'

Kate grabbed her arm. 'Hold tight, Avon, it's a mite rough going just here. The boys will light down and help. We're making for that pass between the rocks, there's a natural break into a valley where there's water and shade trees and where we'll likely camp.'

They clung together as the heavy wagon lurched up the incline and between a rough tumble of rock. Beyond, the hills rose, bleached and sharp-edged against the sky, their slopes covered with yellow pine and scrub. From the valley, they entered another, wider valley with a creek running through it and groves of trees and good grass and here the wagons halted and their dusty, hot occupants tumbled out thankfully to flock into the shade or, in the case of the children, splash in the creek.

Frank had dismounted and thrown his reins to one of the men with him and turned to help Avon down from her seat when Ted remarked,

'What's got into Pheelie? She looks madder'n a kicked cat!'

Avon looked up as Frank swung her to the ground and saw the elder Miss Skellar staring at them and thought Ted's description not ill-fitting. The huge, pale-blue eyes were sparkling dangerously and the high colour in her cheeks was not entirely owing to the heat and the rough ride.

Ted grinned impudently at Frank. 'You'd best go smooth her down 'fore she scratches you.'

'You hold your mouth,' Frank snapped, and walked away.

Ted stared after him. 'What's got him so frothy?'

Avon could not resist saying: 'Perhaps he thinks your sister is annoyed with him about something.'

'It'll be the first time ever. Mostly she's smiling fit to bust when Frank calls—and Ma sends me off picking berries when they're sitting on the porch,' he added gloomily.

So Frank was courting Pheelie, it seemed, and was now going to be scolded for paying attention to another girl. Would he, Avon wondered, plead his interest was solely in hearing news of England, or a kindly wish to make a compatriot feel at home in a strange land? Would he resent Pheelie's possessive attitude?

Avon turned away, determined not to think more about it. Already she had an uneasy suspicion she was thinking too much about Frank Carline. He attracted her, but she did not intend to let the attraction get deeper. If he was Pheelie's beau, then Pheelie was justified in resenting his behaviour on the drive.

The crowd of young men—farmers, cowmen and townsmen—were unloading baskets of food from the wagons and the girls were spreading bright Indian blankets on the grass and chattering like a flock of birds. The valley narrowed at the far end. The sides sloped gently up to bare ridges where rock showed its grim face and no vegetation grew. But the valley was lush and green. Blue lupins and the little pink bitteroot grew on the slopes, and Ted had joined his schoolmates in their hunt for wild raspberries.

The scene was gay and Avon's heart rose in gratitude to her uncle for allowing her to join in the festivities. For a second she had a vision of her aunt as she had seen her standing on the verandah steps, then she brushed it aside.

Food was spread out and disappeared with astonishing rapidity. After the meal, people settled into little groups and the older women brought out their knitting and crochet. The teacher organised races for the exuberant youngsters and Frank and some of the other men were called on to hold the winning tape and give decisions on fairness.

Avon, sitting with Kate, asked: 'Who is that big dark man beside Frank Carline?'

'He's Red Jessup, Frank's foreman.'

'I don't think I like his appearance.'

'You ain't alone there. Red's made enemies since he came here a year since. He drinks hard and folk keep away from him when he's in town on a booze.'

'I wonder Mr Carline keeps him as foreman.'

'I guess he knows his job. Frank's ranch is the richest hereabouts, he's put plenty money into it. He's built himself a fine house and pays his hands well, I guess, from the way they spatter their dough when they visit town.'

A certain langour came over the party. Some of the men wandered off to smoke and 'talk cow' as Kate expressed it. Even the children tired of racing around and amused themselves damming up pools in the creek and floating paper boats. Avon walked over to watch them and found Frank at her side.

'Are you enjoying yourself?' he asked.

She assured him she was, and tried to crush down the pleasure she felt at knowing he had followed her.

'If you'd care to gather some flowers, you can cross the

creek by some stones higher up,' he said, and held out his hand. Without thinking she slipped her hand in his and went with him to where the creek narrowed and flat stones broke the surface of the water. He helped her to cross, but as she put her foot on the last stone it slipped and she would have fallen if he had not caught her up and carried her to the bank. For a moment he held her, looking down into her eyes with an expression that set her heart beating too swiftly for her comfort.

'Thank you,' she said breathlessly, 'I—I nearly slipped.'

'I'm glad you did,' he said softly as he released her. She turned away to hide her agitation—and saw Pheelie Skellar staring at them from the opposite bank with furious eyes!

'Frank, you're wanted,' there was a steely note in Pheelie's voice.

Before Frank could answer Avon said quickly: 'I was going to pick some wildflowers on this side, but it doesn't matter.' She crossed the creek, stepping carefully, aware of Frank's hand on her arm.

'Frank, Ted says his pony's gone lame and will you see to it,' Pheelie smiled at him and for a bare second he hesitated, then nodded and strode off to the picnic ground. As Avon was about to follow, Pheelie put out her hand.

'Wait! You're a stranger here, Avon Meredith, and maybe in England it ain't a low-down, cheap and sneaky thing for a girl to throw herself for all to see at another girl's beau! But we don't hold with such ways here and—'

'Neither do I,' Avon said quietly, holding in her rising temper with an effort. 'I haven't thrown myself at anyone.'

'You have too!' Pheelie's voice rose shrilly. 'You set your mind on Frank the minute you saw him! Making him ride close to you on the ride and dragging him away to help you pick flowers! Flirting with him in a way no decent girl would stoop to do!'

Anger lit in Avon's grey eyes. 'I did not make Mr Carline ride beside me, nor was it *my* suggestion I crossed the creek to pick flowers. He has chosen to show me courtesy and kindness, which is more than you have done!' Suddenly her anger refused to be crushed down any longer. 'To be truthful, you have been both rude and quite excessively silly! If you object to Mr Carline's behaviour, you had better speak to him, had you not?'

For a moment a flash of something vicious showed in Pheelie's eyes.

'You'd best be careful, Avon Meredith,' she said it quietly, but fury throbbed beneath her words. 'You'd best be real careful!'

She swung around and almost ran back to the picnic crowd.

For a few minutes Avon stood still, shaken by the girl's attack and angry with her own outburst. It had been undignified and unwise to answer back. She should have ignored Pheelie's wild accusations, realising they were spawned by jealousy which had spoiled the day for her. Was Frank truly her beau? His behaviour made her doubt it.

She saw Kate coming towards her and went to meet her.

'Avon,' Kate's honest face was slightly pink and she looked flustered, 'I think maybe . . . Would you care to ride back in the Mullers' wagon? I'm sure Mr Muller would be glad to have you and drop you off at the farm. The Skellars' wagon is kind of crowded now Ted has to ride in it on account of his pony going lame.'

'And Pheelie does not want me in the wagon,' Avon said, lifting her chin defiantly. 'Well, I certainly have no wish to go back with her. I'd be pleased to ride back with Mr Muller.'

'Pheelie's got all frothed up, she's been saying things, real nasty things about you, Avon,' Kate said angrily as she took Avon's arm. 'I told her to hush up and was she mad with me!'

'I am afraid we had a—slight difference of opinion, Kate, and she does not like me very much.'

'And I know why,' Kate growled. 'Pheelie Skellar's been pole-cat jealous since you arrived, but don't you pay no heed.'

After the baskets had been repacked and put in the wagons there was a general outcry from the younger folk that it was too early to make for home, and a banjo was produced and a sing-song started, led by the minister.

Avon, her anger cooled but still disturbed, wished she could be alone for a little to sort out her uneasy thoughts, and when Ted came up to her and said he'd been sent to take her across the creek again so she could pick her flowers, she went with him gladly. She crossed safely this time and knowing Ted was longing to get back to the fun, told him to return.

'I'll pick what I want and come back by myself,' she told him. 'What time do we leave, Ted?'

'Six o'clock.'

She wandered along the banks of the creek, letting her thoughs drift and soothed by the sound of rippling water and the breeze rustling through the willows. Further on she caught sight of a bank of wild lupins and she left the creek, making her way through a thicket of scrub. She picked some of the flowers and, seeing a narrow ravine opening off the valley, decided to explore a little. She was out of sight and earshot of the crowd and feeling a gentle peace soothing out the petty irritations of the day. It was only a little after five o'clock so she had plenty of time in which to restore her natural optimism. She refused to let her thoughts dwell on Frank's attentions and Pheelie's resentment of them, and turned her mind to memories of England, her friends there and her happy and secure life before her mother died.

The ravine was narrow, with steep walls rising precipitously on either side. A quail rose out of the mesquite, its cry: 'Queet-queet-queet' startling her for a moment. Overhead, motionless against the imperceptibly fading sky, a hawk hung. Avon stood still, letting the beauty and peace sink into her heart.

A glance at her watch told her she should be returning to the wagons and she began slowly to retrace her steps. She had been away longer than she had thought, but there was still plenty of time. She wondered if Frank would notice she was not on the Skellar wagon—and told herself quickly she did not care if he did or not.

She paused to pick a few more flowers, then crossed the creek and made her way up the bank and past the willows . . . and stood staring at the trampled grass and patch of shade where the horses had been picketed and the empty space where the wagons had stood! They had gone—and she was alone in the Indian Hills with shadows slowly thickening around her and silence broken only by the creek and the distant bark of a coyote!

CHAPTER
FIVE

FOR some minutes Avon stood perfectly still and stared, unable to believe her eyes. It was barely half-past five; what had made the party move off so early? She put her watch to her ear, no, it had not stopped. They had all left early and no one had troubled to call her! Perhaps they had not even missed her.

As her first paralysing astonishment and dismay turned into coherent thought she tried to work out how it could have happened, and she remembered her proposed change of wagon. But why had Mr Muller not noticed her absence? Surely Kate had told him he would have another passenger on the homeward journey? But suppose Kate had forgotten to tell Mr Muller and had told only the Skellars who would have gone off thinking Avon was with Mr Muller who would naturally suppose her to be with the Skellars? It must have happened that way, but it did not explain why the party had left so early. That must have been Ted's fault. Probably he had misunderstood the hour of departure and, engrossed with his friends, had forgotten what he had told her.

Yes, that must have been the way it happened, but knowing the cause did nothing to reduce the shock of finding herself alone in a slowly darkening world of mysterious shadows and sudden, uneasy fears.

How soon would they miss her and come back? If the wagons kept apart, no one would miss her until the main road was reached and someone, Kate perhaps, looked for her to say goodbye.

An eerie sound made her nerves tighten painfully for a second. It was only the note of an owl, but it served to emphasise her solitary state and the empty spaces around her.

'There is nothing to be frightened of,' she said it aloud. 'I must simply wait here until someone comes for me. I am perfectly safe, nothing can harm me . . .' Her voice died away as she remembered Pheelie's laughing rebuke to Frank about bears. *Were* there bears in these hills? She started nervously and looked around her. Surely any animal would have been scared off by the noise of so many humans, they would avoid the valley— unless they wanted water!

Above her the sky held all the glory of a slowly dying sun, but as she waited, a gradual diminishing of richness heralded the approach of evening and she shivered. She might pretend to herself she was brave but she knew she was both chilled and frightened. To wait, alone, in this silent, darkening valley, straining her ears for the sound of rescue . . .

She walked slowly back to the creek and stood watching a paper boat lazily circling in a little whirlpool. How long ago it seemed now that a group of yelling boys had played there. Why had she gone to pick flowers? And why had she not resisted the impulse to wander up the ravine where she was out of earshot of the party? And why had she not asked someone more reliable than Ted about the hour for leaving?

Resolutely she fought back a rising panic. Kate, or one of the girls she knew would not panic. They would not start uneasily at every mysterious sound and feel afraid to look up at the craggy hills where a faint light still lingered.

'I am *not* afraid!' she declared. She dragged her eyes from the creek and stared up at the ridge on the far side of the valley and a startled cry escaped her. High on the ridge, outlined against the faint light, she saw a motionless horseman. The sky rider!

For a second she believed her taut nerves had played a trick on her and that the silent figure, still as if carved from stone, was a hallucination. She stumbled back from the creek, instinctively seeking the shelter of the trees, and saw a faint movement in the still figure and knew he had seen her.

She could do nothing. If she ran away she would certainly get lost. If she did not remain where she was no one would rescue her. She would have to stay. From the shelter of the trees she looked again at the ridge and saw it was empty.

'If he is an outlaw,' she told herself, trying to ignore the beating of her frightened heart, 'he won't come near, he will think there may be others . . . He has to keep away from people . . .' She paused, straining her ears. Was that a faint sound at the end of the valley? The blood drummed in her ears as she waited, tense and shivering. Then it came closer, a horse's hoof striking rock . . . a splashing as a horse crossed the creek higher up. The sky rider had seen her and was coming!

He rode up slowly, glancing from side to side, his big black horse stepping daintily and trying to snatch an occasional mouthful of the lush valley grass. With wide, startled eyes, her hands clasped to her breast, Avon watched him dismount and after another swift look around him, walk towards her. Her light dress made her conspicuous among the shadows, it was that which had given her away when she stood by the creek.

He walked lightly, his high-heeled boots making no sound on the trampled grass around her, and stopped before her, looking at her for a silent moment before saying,

'Miss Meredith. What in hookey do you do out here alone at this time of evening?'

She recognised his voice. 'So you *are* the sky rider? Frank . . . someone said you had gone west.'

'Seems folk take quite an interest in my movements.' His voice was harsh as he stood with his thumbs hooked in his belt, a belt that carried a gun. 'What are you doing here?'

'I came with a picnic party. We camped here. I made a mistake in the time and—and they have gone off and left me.' In spite of herself, her voice wavered.

'How come they didn't miss you?'

'I don't know. It may have been because I was to go back in another wagon and there was some mistake over it. I was across the creek, picking lupins, and then I walked a little way up a ravine—and when I came back they had all gone.' She knew she was near tears.

'Didn't they tell you what time they planned to leave?'

'I was told six, but they must have left before half-past five. Someone will miss me, of course, and return.'

'It could be a matter of some hours if the wagons split up in the dark,' he said, voicing her own fears. 'I guess you know me.'

'Yes, you were on the train—and ran away.'

'I sure had something to run from,' he said grimly. 'You'll know my name too, I reckon.'

There was silence. The big horse, now a dim shape, grazed noisily, his harness clinking as he moved. The owl hooted again and was answered by a far-off mate.

The man said abruptly: 'The cold's rising. I'll get a fire going and make coffee, but not here.'

'I cannot leave the valley,' she protested swiftly, 'if someone comes, I should miss them.'

'You'll get darn cold. There's a plateau up back with pines that will hide smoke if I keep the fire low. You'll come with me.'

'No!' She backed away, her uneasiness growing. 'I—I prefer to stay here.'

'Waiting for a grizzly to come along?' he asked mockingly. 'You're coming out of this valley with me.' He whistled and the horse raised its head enquiringly and then came towards them.

'I refuse to go with you!' she cried, and felt herself caught up and placed none too gently on the back of the big horse. A second later, Grant was in the saddle and she was forced to cling to him as they crossed the creek and rode up the ravine where the ground became rough.

Fear swept her in icy waves. He was a murderer, a man hunted by the law! One of the badmen Texas had told her about. A man who obeyed no laws but those of his own desires. His behaviour in the train had been grossly impertinent, but she had not felt this chilling fear of him. Where was he taking her? If a rescue party came, how would they find her?

His body felt hard as steel. His wide shoulders blocked her view but she could feel the horse scrambling up-wards, surefooted as a mountain goat, and then turn to the right where trees closed over them, shutting out most of the waning light.

Grant dismounted and swung her off the horse.

'Guess this'll have to do,' he said as he began to unstrap a burlap bag from the saddle, 'I don't have anything but coffee and crackers, but they're better than nothing. A fire will warm us—and keep off the grizzlies. Gather up some dry sticks and brush.'

Nervously she obeyed, catching up pieces of dry brushwood and twigs. She watched him make a fire, carefully coaxing it to glow rather than smoke. He had found larger bits of wood and once the fire was red, he filled a battered tin coffee pot with water and coffee and set it on the embers and opened a packet of crackers.

She lingered in the shadows, wondering if she could slip away without his noticing. As if he guessed her thoughts, he turned his head to say abruptly,

'Come over to the fire.'

'No, I—I'd rather not.'

His lean jaw tightened. 'Want me to fetch you?'

As he started to rise, she came forward, knowing he meant to carry out his threat.

The fire warmed her chilled body. After a moment's hesitation she accepted the mug of coffee he offered and was grateful for the strength and courage it gave her. When she had finished, he filled the mug for himself, and offered her the crackers.

The moon had risen, but its light filtered only fitfully through the pines. By the glow of the fire, she looked at the man who had treated her in so summary a manner. The firelight picked out the strong, stern planes of his tanned face and the shadowed eyes bent broodingly upon the flickering flames. He looked thinner than when she had last seen him and something bleak and harsh in his face did nothing to lessen her uneasiness.

He looked up and caught her eyes upon him. 'Reckon this doesn't match up with picnic food, Miss Meredith.'

'How do you know my name?' she demanded. A spark of anger was growing inside her. He was treating her abominably and she would not let him see she was afraid!

'Saw it, with the address you were going to, on the label on your grip in the train that time. Was Haskin with you today?' He shot the question at her.

'No.' She stared defiantly at him across the fire, 'but he is in the vicinity. He called at my uncle's farm a few days ago. He is looking for you.'

He tossed a stick into the fire. 'Did he say why?'

'He didn't have to,' she said coldly, 'I saw a poster in Miles City.'

'Did Haskin add any fancy touches to it?' She heard the mockery in his words and stiffened angrily.

'Only that you shot and killed an unarmed man and there was a witness, and later, you broke jail. Sheriff Haskin knew you were on the train that day.'

'And you told him how I'd slipped off into that little valley.'

'I *ought* to have told him, I know.'

'So you didn't? Now why was that, Miss Avon Meredith?'

She bit her lip. 'I . . . Well, I had no way of knowing then you were the man he was looking for. Had I known—'

'You'd have handed me over to the law, as was your duty, and collected the reward.' He smiled, but his eyes remained watchful and cold. 'Maybe I'd better not let you go back to your folk. Haskin will be mighty interested in what you can tell him, I reckon.'

She caught her breath. 'But—you cannot keep me here, a prisoner! Besides, people will come looking for me, they may be here already.'

'Maybe they are.' He rose in a sudden, easy motion. 'Reckon I'll take a look-see.' He strode away and was lost in shadows.

The fire died to a few red embers which made the surrounding darkness more mysterious and sinister and she glanced around nervously when he did not return, her ears pricked for strange sounds, her eyes searching the shadows. *Was* there something moving between the trees . . . ? She rose, her breath catching in her throat as her eyes tried to pierce the darkness. A stone rattled. Surely that was the pad of a soft foot . . . A snuffling sound brought panic. Texas had once said something about mountain lions! She caught sight of a tall figure and ran to him, grasping his arm as she stammered,

'I—I heard something over there . . . A step—and a strange noise . . . Oh! There it is again!' In her terror she pressed close to him and felt his arms around her. When he spoke, laughter lay under his words.

'Darkie sure can make odd sounds when he's a mind to, pawing the ground and whistling soft through his nostrils.'

She gasped and felt colour rush to her face. 'You mean it was your horse?'

'Yes, ma'am. Horses don't have good manners where ladies are concerned. Did you reckon it was a wild animal?'

'I—yes, I did. Pheelie Skellar said something to Frank Carline about bears and Texas—'

'Frank Carline?' he asked sharply.

'Yes, he's the owner of the Two-Bar ranch. I am sure he will return to find me. Please let me go back to the valley. I—I will promise not to tell anyone I met you.'

He was still holding her and as she looked up at him she saw the laughter die out of his eyes.

'And let a murderer go free?' His voice was hard.

'*Was* the man unarmed?' She was not certain why she asked it.

He shrugged. 'I believe so.'

'And you did kill him?'

'A man swore to it.'

'But surely you must know if you shot the man—or if the witness is lying and trying to incriminate you?'

'Sure I know—and I'm aiming to know plenty more.' His arms tightened around her and something in his face made her heart leap and fear return. As she strained away from him, he released her and, turning, he strode to the fire and stamped it out with a booted foot.

'I reckon we'll save Carline a ride,' he spoke over his shoulder. 'I'll take you to your uncle's farm.'

He went to where his horse was picketed, leaving her to stare after him. Could she trust him? Surely he did not mean to risk capture by leaving the hills that hid him so well?

As he came up with Darkie, she said impulsively: 'If we should meet someone who is looking for me . . . it would not be safe for you.'

He smiled wryly. 'I'm not aiming to meet up with Carline or Haskin; I'll ride another trail.' He helped her mount Darkie and stood a moment, looking up at her. 'You scared?'

She drew herself up indignantly. 'Certainly not! I shall be very grateful to you if you will take me home—and I shall not say I met you.'

'You've sure got grit,' he said slowly, 'just like when you knocked that fellow's hand up in the train. Keep tight hold of me, the trail I'm taking is a rough one.'

Once more she found herself clinging to the man Sheriff Haskin had declared a cold-blooded killer as Darkie picked his way through the pines and down into a narrow canyon. Sometimes the big horse slipped and sent a rattle of stones down and she tried not to gasp. For a time it was light enough to see the stark walls rising above them, then cloud covered the moon, but the horse seemed to know his way and at last they had reached the foothills and were on more level ground.

Grant did not speak and she guessed he was listening, as she was, for the sound of another horseman. She could not recognise the trail they were taking. As he had warned, the going was rough and she began to feel desperately weary. Fear still lingered; she had only his word that he was taking her to her uncle's farm. By now she had lost all sense of direction. The shadowy clumps of trees and brush, low hills and occasional shallow creek were unreal, part of a frightening dream. Suddenly they were out into open land and she felt the horse's muscles move under her as he began to gallop, his great stride eating up the ground.

This was where danger lay! There was no shelter and the moon shone high above them, painting the land with silver light and purple shadow. She became aware of Grant's swift glances to right and left and she grew tense with apprehension. If Haskin should be abroad . . . Both men carried guns and there would be a fight!

Suddenly she recognised the field they were crossing. The farmhouse lay ahead and she could see a light through the willows bordering the creek. Grant reined in abruptly and was off the horse and had lifted her down before she knew what was happening.

'There's a light in the house, maybe your folks are waiting up for you,' he said.

She pulled her dazed thoughts together, aware of aching muscles and deep desire for sleep.

'Thank you for bringing me back, I am truly grateful to you. Now please go quickly, it is not safe for you to stay here.'

He did not answer. He stood, his thumbs hooked in his gun belt, staring down at her. His hat, pulled low, kept his face in shadow and she could not read his expression, but her heart suddenly began to beat unevenly and her breath quickened as she drew back.

'Wait!' He caught her arm. 'I guess I owe you an apology for the way I behaved in the train that time.'

'Please say no more,' she said coldly, 'I—I have not thought of it since.'

She heard his quick intake of breath before he said: 'Maybe you haven't . . . but I guess I have!'

He grabbed her, crushing her slight body against him as his mouth found hers in a hard, fierce kiss, a kiss that was almost cruel in its demanding passion and set the moonlit world spinning around her! She struggled but was held in arms of steel! He kissed her again, and again, her mouth, her eyes, her cheeks! With a quick movement he pulled down the neck of her dress and she shivered as she felt his lips on the little hollow beneath her throat.

'Let me go!' she whispered wildly, 'Oh please . . . let me go!'

He released her so abruptly she would have fallen if he had not caught her arm and steadied her. Her weariness and bruised and aching body were forgotten, swallowed up in the tumultuous beating of her heart and a burning fire that ran through her veins.

'Maybe you'll have that to think about now . . . and maybe I shouldn't have done it!' He spoke harshly. 'I'm not a liar so I'm not saying I'm sorry!' Suddenly his voice dropped and he whispered: 'Oh God, it's sweet to kiss you . . .'

He was mounted and jerking the horse's head around before she could move or speak. Darkie sprang forward under the prick of the spur. As Avon watched, her hands clasped to her breast, thin cloud misted the moon's light and slowly the soft thud of hooves died away and she was alone. He had gone back to the hills, to hide and to keep watch from the bare ridges. The lone Sky Rider!

CHAPTER
SIX

'Avon! Thank God!' Frank Carline slid from his horse and came up the verandah steps at a run. 'What happened? How did you get back? Are you all right?'

'Child, you've given us a bad scare,' Ben said, putting his hand on Avon's arm. Rita, standing in the background, was silent, with an odd expression as she stared at Avon.

'I am perfectly all right, thank you, Uncle Ben—but I *am* dreadfully tired.' She made an effort to pull herself out of the turmoil of feeling which Grant's kiss had aroused in her. 'I waited in the valley. Then a—a man came and I rode behind him and he brought me back.'

'What man?' Frank asked, his handsome face full of concern. 'Where did he come from? Did you know him?'

'No. I think he said he was a prospector. He gave me some coffee.' She wondered where the words had come from so easily. 'He was quite old—and very kind. He left me at the back field and rode away.'

'How did it happen?' Frank demanded. 'Why were you left? I was told you were in the Mullers' wagon. We led the train because Pheelie wanted to get back quickly and I didn't check out that you were with the Mullers.'

'Yes, I'd like to know just how you came to be abandoned and no one missed you,' her uncle's voice was stern. 'Seems to me, some people have been mighty careless. Weren't you there when the party packed up, Avon?'

'No. I was told they were to leave at six and when I came back from picking wildflowers at half past five, they had all left.'

'Who told you?' Frank asked.

'I—I forget. It was a mistake. I was to return with the Mullers who thought I was with the Skellars.'

'Carline only realised you were missing when he called in to see if you'd got back and weren't too tired,' Ben said. 'He and I were about to set off to find you. I'm mighty glad to see you back, Avon.' For the first time she was aware of affection in her uncle's voice. 'We'll get you something to eat.'

'She's too tuckered out to eat,' Rita said abruptly, 'she'll go to bed before she drops.' She moved to the door and Avon followed her into the bedroom. She was dimly aware of her aunt helping to undress her, then she sank into blessed oblivion.

The sun was high when she awoke next morning. Her muscles were stiff and she winced when she moved. She lay, letting memories rush over her. How dared Ken Grant insult her so! To snatch her and kiss her against her will as no man had kissed her ever before! She would never forgive him, never!

Yet as she thought of the past night, insensibly her outraged feelings began to fade. She had been alone with him, a lawless man, and completely in his power. He had behaved disgracefully, of course, but he had not harmed her, and he *had* brought her home when it meant danger for him, danger that he might be captured and danger that she would set Sheriff Haskin on his trail.

Did he trust her to keep her promise? She had defied the law by concealing her meeting with a hunted criminal and it was her duty to tell the sheriff, but she knew she would keep silent.

She was startled to find herself thinking less harshly of Ken Grant. She could not forgive him and she did not wish ever to meet him again, but she was finding it difficult to see him as a ruthless killer. The harshness in his face, the sudden tensing of nerves, the brooding silences were the results of constantly watching, lack of sleep and perhaps food.

He could not hide for ever in those inhospitable hills. Perhaps even now he was riding west, his great black horse putting a safe distance between him and his pursuers. The thought brought relief. She knew that in spite of her indignation at his treatment of her, she did not want Ken Grant to be hunted to the death.

She dressed and went into the kitchen where Rita was preparing chicken food.

Her aunt turned to say,

'I heard you move. The coffee's fresh and bacon and beans keeping hot.'

'Thank you, Aunt Rita.'

'You'd best rest up today,' her aunt said in the same dry voice. 'You'll likely be muscle-sore after your ride.' She picked up the bowl and went out.

As she ate, Avon thought of the coffee and crackers she had shared with Ken Grant and wondered how he got supplies of food. Did he take a chance and ride into some small town or had he a cache somewhere in the hills?

Later in the morning her uncle came into the kitchen where she was ironing a dress and asked her how she felt, and again expressed indignation at the carelessness that might have had unhappy consequences.

'*Are* there bears in the Indian Hills, Uncle Ben?' she asked.

'There might be a few, but there's worse than bears. To my mind there's a good chance the rustlers who've been plaguing us have their hide-out somewhere deep in those hills. It wouldn't have been good for you to meet them.'

Avon shivered as a sudden chill touched her. She remembered the train hold-up and the evil face of the robber when his mask had slipped. Men who pitted themselves against the law would have no standards of behaviour where women were concerned.

'I'm going into Sweetwater to see about hiring extra help now the corn's ripe and oats coming up,' Ben said.

'Guess I'll take something to eat on the way.' He went to a cupboard and pulled out a tin and peered into it. 'What in hookey does Rita want to make burnt-sugar cake for? She knows I don't like it.' He put the tin back and proceeded to cut himself a thick sandwich of bread and sausage while Avon watched with wide eyes.

'Did you say you *don't* like burnt-sugar cake, Uncle Ben?'

'Never could abide it, too sweet for my taste. Rita hasn't baked it for years. Anything you want in Sweetwater, Avon?'

She shook her head, her thoughts in a whirl. Rita had not baked her cake for Ben, she had baked it for the picnic but had been to proud to admit it after all she had said about the waste of time and foolishness of the day's outing. And when she had offered it, it had been abruptly, cruelly refused! Avon spun around and ran out of the room.

'Aunt Rita!' She was breathless when she ran up to Rita as she knelt weeding the vegetable patch. 'I—I'm sorry I was so rude when you offered me your cake yesterday. I thought you really didn't want me to have it, that Uncle Ben had made you offer it.'

Rita rose, wiping her hands on her apron. 'Ben said he weren't feeling hungry right then so I reckoned it needn't go to waste if you took it.' She kept her face averted, staring across the sunlit fields of corn and oats.

'It was very kind of you, Aunt Rita, and I was perfectly horrid. Please forgive me.' The picture of Rita holding the rejected cake as she watched the wagonload of lively young people drive away came back to fill her with remorse. 'Please, can I have some of your cake at dinner? It looks delicious.'

'Reckon you can have all of it,' Rita turned to the house. 'Ben don't eat cake much.'

'But don't you like it, Aunt Rita?' Avon asked, walking beside her.

Rita shrugged her thin shoulders. 'Time's past when I

bother what I eat.' They had reached the back porch before she added reluctantly; 'Once was my favourite cake for sure.'

'Then we'll both enjoy it,' Avon told her gaily. 'Let's have some more coffee and some cake right now. I'm still hungry.'

She made the coffee and cut the cake and brought it to the verandah where Rita sat rocking in a manner most unusual for her.

'I don't know what in this world I'm doing behaving ladylike with coffee and cake mid-morning when there's a heap of work to be done,' she remarked.

'It is good for you to rest sometimes,' Avon told her, 'you work too hard, Aunt Rita.'

There was a silence while they drank coffee. Suddenly Rita said, staring straight ahead.

'Guess that's all I'm good for, hard work.'

'Aunt Rita, that isn't true.' Avon bent forward and impulsively touched the work-roughened hand lying in Rita's lap. The hand was not withdrawn as she went on eagerly, 'You've made a happy home for Uncle Ben, and you've helped to make the farm a fine one. You've nursed sick neightbours, I know.'

'I do mighty little else worth while . . . and I don't like change.'

Avon sighed. 'I realise I have made a great change in your life. You must have resented a stranger coming to live with you, I am afraid.'

Rita rose and shook out her skirts before turning to the door. She paused to look back with the suspicion of a smile touching her thin lips, 'I reckon you could have been worse.'

After supper, Ben had the business of hiring extra help to discuss with Rita and Avon went out to the back yard where she found Texas peacefully sitting on a tree stump smoking a cigarette.

'Heard how you got yourself lost in the hills yester-day,' he greeted her. 'Seems to me there's plenty other folk they could have left adrift without picking on you. How come, Avon?'

She seated herself beside him and told him of the mix up about which wagon she was to ride in, and the mistake about the time of departure. Texas was a good listener and she found herself describing the picnic and the people she had met.

'Well, it's my guess Miss Pheelie Skellar don't take kindly to Frank cutting you out of the herd,' he said shrewdly, making her laugh.

'I am afraid you *may* be right. She did come after me and send Frank back to see to Ted's pony which had gone lame.'

He nodded. 'Ted was over early this morning to borrow some horse liniment. He was kind of upset about yesterday and said as how you could have missed getting back because of a mistake he'd made in the time.'

'Well, yes. I didn't want to get him into trouble, but it *was* Ted who told me they were to leave at six o'clock.'

Texas dropped the butt of his cigarette and ground it into the earth.

'And who told Ted?'

'I don't know, I suppose he just thought it was six.'

Texas snorted. 'Six nothing! Pheelie told him.'

'Pheelie?' she repeated, startled.

'Sure. Why did you go plucking flowers a second time?'

'Ted took me, he said he had been sent to help me. I thought it must have been Frank who sent him.'

'Mebbe I'm riding the wrong line, but I'd be mighty interested to know did young Frank send Ted with that message.'

Avon swung around to stare at him as his meaning burst upon her.

'Texas, you don't mean . . . You can't mean Pheelie . . .'

'Did you and Pheelie part kind of loving when she'd roped Frank off?'

'I—well she *was* rather angry, and quite rude, I'm afraid.' Avon had a sudden vision of Pheelie's furious face and the spiteful flash in her blue eyes as she said: 'You'd best be very careful . . .' Surely her jealousy would not have driven her to such a cruel trick? 'I won't believe it!' she declared impetuously. 'She wouldn't do such a thing to me. It was a mistake; I expect she forgot to correct Ted about the time.'

'And forgot to tell any folk you'd gone over the creek.'

She couldn't have known I was there—unless someone told her.'

'Ted told her,' Texas said grimly, 'and was told to hush up.'

Avon jumped up. 'Don't say anything about it, please. You are only guessing and anyway, it turned out well.'

'I reckon my guesses has a way of turning out right, Ma'am, but like as you say, you didn't come to no harm. A prospector picked you up, you said? Riding single and carrying nothing heavy?'

'Only coffee pot and some crackers.'

Texas proceeded to roll himself another cigarette. 'Kind of greenhorn, I reckon,' he did not look at Avon and his drawl became more pronounced as he went on: 'Prospecting men usually need a heap of tinware and take a burro along to carry it.'

'I—I didn't notice. Perhaps he had left it somewhere —where he had been digging.'

He rose lazily. 'First time I heard of anything worth digging in them hills,' he remarked, and walked away.

Avon watched him go, feeling uneasy. Texas was no fool. Not only did he suspect Pheelie was responsible for the picnic incident, but he did not accept her story of the kindly old prospector. However, something told her he would not speak of his suspicions to anyone.

Some days after this Frank rode over to invite the Merediths to his ranch. Somewhat to Avon's surprise, Ben accepted and Rita did not object beyond saying the hired men would undoubtedly cut off work the moment she and Ben left the farm.

'It's a Sunday,' Frank reminded her, smiling.

'I've never held it to be sinful to work on the Lord's day,' she told him tartly.

'The commandments—'

'Moses was a man, and a man can make mistakes mighty easy. Ben and I will go in the buggy and Avon can ride now she's all set up to be a horsewoman.'

'Doug Haskin said he might ride over on Sunday,' Ben reminded her.

Frank gathered up his reins. 'Bring him along, maybe he'll have news of the rustlers.'

Now there were two hired men to feed, Avon was kept busy. But she still had time to go over her experience in the Indian Hills and wonder, again, if Ken Grant was still there and if the sheriff suspected it and considered Grant to be working with the rustlers. None of the hauls had been spectacular, just a steady draining of herds from many of the big ranches south of the city. Sheriff Haskin had said it was the work of a clever brain behind an experienced gang of thieves. *Was* Grant a rustler as well as a killer? He had not denied the crime to her, he had said there had been a witness to the saloon shooting. But witnesses could be wrong. In a saloon brawl among drunken men, who could be certain of what happened? Grant had made a mistake in breaking jail; he would have stood a better chance of proving a witness wrong if he had fought the charge.

It struck her she was assuming him innocent, despite evidence against it. He had not said he was innocent, but why should he? Why should he care what she thought of him? As she lay in her narrow bed, watching moonlight filter through the curtains, she tried to find the reason why she resisted the idea that Ken Grant was a callous killer.

'I do not believe he meant to kill,' she thought. 'It could have been an accident, a dreadful mistake. Texas says most men won't shoot unless the other man draws first, unless they have to defend themselves. I don't think Ken Grant is a ruthless killer.'

Daisy Skellar rode over to see Avon. Rita brought coffee and stood, her hands on her hips, listening to them.

'It was just *awful*, you being left behind like that at the picnic,' Daisy said earnestly. 'I felt real bad about it when I heard. You must have been scared, Avon.'

'Yes, I was, Daisy.'

'It was lucky nothing worse'n scaring happened to her,' Rita snapped. 'Those hills hold more than wild-flowers and jack rabbits. It don't tally with me her being taken to pick flowers and getting the wrong time for leaving. Seems likely someone didn't want her along.'

Avon put down her cup hastily. Did Rita, too, suspect she had been deliberately left behind? She glanced at Daisy and saw how the colour had risen in her face and she said quickly,

'It was really my fault, I ought to have been more careful. I certainly will, next time.'

'Next time,' Rita gave Daisy a long, hard look before turning to go, 'you'd best ride both ways in the Mullers' wagon.'

There followed an uncomfortable pause while Avon searched for a safer topic.

'Daisy, I think you once told me of a seamstress in Sweetwater who sometimes made gowns for you.'

Daisy nodded. 'Sure, Amelia Oakley. She lives over Smith's Mercantile. She can't do fancy work but she's neat and fits well. Why? Are you getting a dress made?'

'Yes. At least, I hope I can get it made.' Avon did not elaborate. There was no need to tell Daisy for whom the dress would be made—if it ever *was* made.

That evening Rita turned from washing the dishes to stare belligerently at Avon.

'What in land's sake would I want a new dress for? If

you've got the notion I'm prinking myself up for a visit to
Frank Carline's outfit on Sunday—'

'I think it is time you had a new dress, Aunt Rita,'
Avon said firmly. 'Muller's have some pretty new dress
goods and Miss Oakley will make it for you.'

'I've got a new dress, my red alpaca.'

'You told me it was eight years old.'

'That's new enough for me. I don't take no interest in
clothes 'cept to keep warm.'

'But I think you *should* take an interest,' Avon persisted. 'I am sure Uncle Ben would like to see you in a
smart new dress, and *I* would like to see you in something pretty.'

'And you're supposing your likes and dislikes can
make me change my mind?'

'Yes. Maybe it is presumptuous of me, but I think you
do like me to want to see you looking elegantly dressed,
Aunt Rita.'

Rita, her hands in the pan of soapy water, stared at
her. For a long moment their eyes met. Avon waited,
wondering if she had touched some tiny vein of feminine
vanity in her aunt.

'You can go into town with Texas tomorrow, when he
takes in a load,' Rita turned back to the dishpan, 'and
see if Fritz Muller keeps anything fit for a decent woman
to wear. And tell Amelia Oakley I'll have no fancy
fixings on it. Take a dress of mine so's she'll have my fit.
Ben'll give you money. And now you can get them
chickens plucked and emptied and quit wasting my
time!'

'Yes, Aunt Rita.' Avon bent her head to hide a smile.
So there *was* a spark of womanly vanity buried deep
under Rita's harsh exterior.

When she climbed aboard the wagon next morning,
Texas remarked on her dress, a blue gingham with tiny
ruffles trimming neck and sleeves.

'You sure do pretty up the scenery around here,'
Avon.'

'I won't be the only one,' she said, and told him of her mission.

Texas opened his eyes wide. 'You sure got sand, Avon, to suggest it! Rita can be tetchy as a teased snake if you go agin her.'

'I didn't, she really wanted a nice new gown but she would not admit it.'

Mr Muller greeted her as an old friend and got out his new dress goods.

'Real Paris fashions, Miss Meredith, you'll not get better in Miles City.'

She chose a rose foulard lightly checked with grey, knowing the colour would suit her aunt's eyes and hair. Amelia Oakley was at home and promised to do her best to have the dress ready for the visit to the Two-Bar ranch.

The little town was hot and dusty. Brilliant sunlight showed up peeling paint, sun-warped sidewalks and faded awnings as Avon walked to the livery stables to meet Texas. Above her a 'Barber and Dentist' sign creaked in the occasional puff of breeze that raised little dust whirls in the wide, almost empty street. A horse hitched to the rail outside a saloon drooped its head wearily, two hens scratched in the dust before the grain store and a small boy pressed his nose against a store window displaying jars of sticky candy.

As she approached the Farmer's Bank, Pheelie Skellar came out of the door. She saw Avon and ducked back quickly. Avon walked on, giving no sign she had noticed the hasty retreat. If Pheelie did not want to meet her, she had no intention of letting her imagine she cared. Probably Pheelie was still feeling jealous—and guilty.

She was quiet on the drive home and Texas, after glancing at her from under his sweat-stained Stetson, asked suddenly,

'You got something on your mind, Avon?'

She moved her shoulders, feeling the hot sun burn through the thin cotton. She had been trying to make up her mind about something; now she came to a decision and turned to the man beside her.

'Texas, what have you heard about the man who is wanted by the law for a killing in a saloon somewhere south, a man called Ken Grant?'

'The man Doug Haskin is trailing?' Texas slapped the reins on the horse's rump reflectively. 'Haskin reckons he's come this way. He broke jail in Laramie and ain't been seen much since. Shot a man dead, they say.'

'How did it happen?'

'Seems there was some trouble in a saloon and a young cowhand called Jones got in the way of a bullet. He weren't armed, which makes things look bad for Grant who, like most gents in that city, had kept his gun handy. The bartender swore he saw Grant kill Jones.'

'Do you think he could have made a mistake, Texas?'

Texas did not answer at first. Handing the reins to Avon, he proceeded to roll himself a cigarette. When it was lit and he had resumed driving, he said,

'You got a reason for asking?'

She hesitated, uncertain if she could trust him with the truth. He guessed her thought and drawled, keeping his eyes on the patiently jogging horse,

'Don't say nothing if you'd rather. I can keep things under my hat, but—'

'I know I can trust you, Texas. I—I met Ken Grant on the train when it was robbed . . .' She told him of the hold-up and the attempt to steal her watch and how she had knocked the man's gun up, and Grant's swift and stealthy exit from the train.

'Sheriff Haskin said Grant probably got a horse and he may be hiding in this part of the territory.'

Texas whistled softly. 'And you said nothing 'bout this to Haskin, I guess.'

'No. Grant may be guilty, but I did not want to put the law on his trail.'

'Or let out you know for sure he's holed up in the Indian Hills.'

She caught her breath. 'Why do you say that? No one has seen him.'

'A rider's been seen agin the skyline more'n once. The Indians call him the sky rider and he's on a big nigger horse. Grant bought a black Oregon cayuse after he'd left the train. It's my guess he's in the hills right now.' He looked at her, his face suddenly stern. 'I reckon you met him when you got forgotten on that picnic, you sure didn't make that prospector man sound genuine.'

She nodded, meeting his eyes squarely. 'He rescued me. He lit a fire and shared his coffee and crackers with me and rode me back to the farm. I wasn't going to let anyone know. He risked a lot to bring me back.'

'Sure did,' Texas agreed. 'Haskin's taking the war path. There's too much crime around these days, rustling and train hold-ups, and a bank robbed in Miles City last week and a teller hurt.'

'Do *you* think Grant is also concerned in these crimes, Texas?'

'Aw heck, Avon, who's to know that? A man as does one crime don't usually mind taking a hand in another. If Grant killed a man—'

'You say "if",' she interrupted swiftly. '*Do* you think he shot the man Jones?'

Texas jerked the reins. 'I ain't believing nothing yet. But me, I'd want more than the word of a Mexican barkeep before I'd give a man the leading part in a necktie party.'

Neither spoke again until Texas pulled up before the big barn. Avon sat for a moment, her hands in her lap, then she said slowly,

'Guilty or not guilty, why does Grant stay where he has been seen and where the sheriff hunts him? Why doesn't he ride north, or to the Rockies where he would be safe?'

'Maybe he's looking for something here.'

'Looking for what?'

'The truth, I reckon.'

'What sort of truth?'

'The truth about what happened that night in Tony's saloon in Laramie.'

'Texas! You know the place?'

'Never been there in my life,' he said shortly, and drove the wagon into the shed.

CHAPTER
SEVEN

Avon tried to persuade herself the visit to the ranch was not important to her, and failed. She found herself thinking of Frank rather too often for comfort as the day drew near. She remembered how his dark eyes had caught and held hers on the day of the Skellars' party and the odd little shock that had run through her, and wondered if it had been a premonition of a deeper liking for the handsome young rancher who had shown enough interest in her to make Pheelie jealous. Frank was a man not easy to forget, there was a strength and resolution lying under his easy, pleasant manner. His face, when he had asked her who the man was who had rescued her, had been suddenly hard and the look in his eyes had startled her.

When she had first met Frank she had thought him rather too young and easy-mannered to manage successfully the tough outfit of cowpunchers needed on a ranch, but she had changed her mind. Frank knew how to handle men, even his unprepossessing foreman, Red Jessup.

Sheriff Haskin rode up to the house after breakfast on Sunday and Ben told him he was welcome to ride with them to the Two-Bar ranch.

'Come up and take coffee,' Ben invited from his seat on the verandah, 'while the womenfolk prink themselves and take a week over it. Avon's persuaded Rita to get a new dress. Don't know how she's done it, I've tried many a time. Usually Rita doesn't bother with such things.'

Avon peeped out the screen door. 'We shall *not* take a

week, Uncle Ben! And Aunt Rita looks really elegant in her dress—and don't you men forget to tell her so.'

Haskin pulled off his hat as he came up the steps. 'If you'll guarantee I won't get my ears blistered, Miss Avon. I've never known your aunt welcome a compliment.'

'Perhaps they have not been the right ones.' Avon smiled at him before going back to her 'prinking'. She felt glad he was to ride with them. She liked his straightforward manner and air of quiet authority and the slow smile that could lighten the sternness of his face.

She found Rita standing before her looking-glass. Amelia Oakley had done her work well. The pleating on the bodice, and the skirt, slightly looped at the back, gave a fullness to Rita's spare figure, and the colour was becoming and seemed to have given a faint rosy glow to her aunt's cheeks.

'Aunt Rita, you look splendid, truly you do!' Avon exclaimed. 'I like your hair plaited around your head like that, you look much younger.'

Rita swung around, her eyes snapping. 'There's no cause for you to crow now you've got me trussed up so's I can hardly breathe! Waste of time and money, that's what it is. Time is past when I cared to look younger.'

She stalked out of the room. As Avon was about to follow her, a slip of something red on the dressing-table caught her eye. She moved the hair brush to find two crumpled geranium petals lying under it! Rita might deny wanting to appear younger but she had not disdained staining her cheeks with very becoming colour!

When Rita rustled onto the verandah, Ben's eyebrows climbed.

'Well, Rita, you've certainly done yourself proud.'

'Don't you go putting the blame on me,' she said sharply. 'Avon teased me sick till she got me spragged out like a spring chicken. You can quit staring, Sheriff—and you, too, Texas. Land's sakes! I ain't seen so many open mouths since I fed the hogs!' She got into the buggy and sat staring stiffly ahead.

They set off with Sheriff Haskin riding beside them. Avon chose to ride in the buggy, having decided the riding skirt and boots her aunt had given her were not suitable for the occasion. The dusty road wound between low green hills, past farms and across dry creek beds and through cottonwood and willow groves.

Frank came to meet them and to swing Avon down from the buggy. She had a little rush of pleasure when she saw him and felt how his hands lingered around her slim waist for a moment longer than was necessary. There was no mistaking the admiration in his eyes and she was glad she had chosen to wear one of her English dresses, a primrose muslin, and a jaunty little flowered hat.

The house was a long, low, white building with a wide roof and with the inevitable verandah running along the front. Inside, the rooms had a richness and elegance that surprised her. Dark panelled walls were hung with paintings, Indian rugs were spread on the polished floor and the furniture carved in the Spanish style gave an air of luxury that did not fit in with her preconceived ideas of a ranch house. A Chinese servant entered and bowed as he served cool drinks to the visitors.

'Glad you could come, Haskin,' Frank said. 'Are you taking a holiday from crime in Miles City?'

'Maybe I am. My deputy's in charge up there right now.'

'Have you come to find out who's rustling our cattle?'

'Could be,' Haskin said briefly. 'What's this talk about a sky rider?'

For a second Avon's heart skipped a beat as she sat looking at the two men.

Frank shrugged. 'Some people lay claim to have seen a horseman against the skyline. The Indians think he's a spirit. He isn't your man, Haskin, no law-breaker would show himself so plainly.'

'You could have the right of it,' the sheriff agreed.

When the visitors had rested from their drive, Frank took them out to the corral used for breaking in wild horses to be used for range work. Cowpunchers were perched along the rails like so many crows, smoking and making derisive remarks to one of their number who was looking anything but happy astride a wild-eyed horse who bucked, arching his back and coming down stiff-legged, a most uncomfortable proceeding for his unfortunate rider.

'Zed's sure got himself a gut-twister,' a puncher said with a grin. 'Hi, Zed, quit waltzing the lady and show the company some rough riding!'

'I'm mighty glad I'm not astride that devil,' the sheriff remarked as the maddened horse twirled about. 'See him swap ends! Your man's hugging the rawhide well, Carline.'

'Zed's a good buster,' Frank agreed.

They watched the display for a time. Suddenly the blown horse stood still, quivering and stretching his neck to get breath. Avon felt pity for the winded, beaten animal who was once wild and free to roam the rangelands.

Frank, watching her, guessed her thoughts and she felt his hand on her arm as he murmured.

'It isn't as cruel as it looks. Once he's gentled, he'll make a good range horse and be treated well. I'm sorry if it has upset you, Avon.'

She looked away, disturbed by what she saw in his dark eyes, and saw the sheriff staring at them, his brows drawn into a frown before he turned abruptly and walked off.

Lunch was good and surprisingly sophisticated. Frank admitted he got frequent supplies from the city and employed a Chinese cook who had once lived in the east.

Avon saw Rita's eyes taking note of everything as the meal progressed, and when they retired to a back room to 'freshen up', Rita touched the big flower-patterned bowl into which the Chinese servant had poured water for them to wash and remarked,

'English porcelain I'll be bound, and them hand towels never come out of Muller's store.' She sniffed. 'Frank Carline sure knows how to throw his money about.'

'He does seem to have rather extravagant tastes,' Avon agreed. She was enjoying her visit even more than she had anticipated. The luxury around her was very delightful after her uncle's farm with its bare minimum comfort. Frank had shown her watercolours of English scenery and there were book-cases filled with imported volumes which he begged her to borrow whenever she liked. He had been at her side most of the day and she could not help noticing Sheriff Haskin's face grow more grim and his conversation more monosyllabic as she talked and laughed with their host.

Red Jessup had come up to speak to Frank when they were watching the bronco-busting and Avon decided she disliked him more than ever. A dangerous man, she thought, hot-tempered and ruthless, and again she wondered why Frank should employ such a man as foreman.

Rita demanded to see the small flower garden Frank had made.

'It sure is pretty,' she admitted grudgingly as she looked at the neat flowerbeds and smooth little lawn, 'but it seems kind of wasteful.'

'Oh, Aunt Rita, it is delightful!' Avon exclaimed, her grey eyes alight with pleasure. 'It reminds me of England. Was that why you made it?'

Frank nodded. 'I don't think it is wasteful if it gives me pleasure. An old Indian looks after it.'

'You sure wouldn't get a cowpuncher looking after them beds,' Rita remarked, her eyes lingering on the bright display.

The bunkhouse was some way from the big house and when they sauntered back, Avon noticed a man come out and swing himself onto a horse. As he rode past, he glanced at the party and Avon had a shock of horrified recognition as she saw the ugly birthmark staining one cheek. He rode on; obviously he had not recognised her—but she knew him! He was the hold-up man in the train, one of the Blackface gang! And he was posing as a ranch hand, working for Frank and planning . . . what? Robbery? Rustling? Or perhaps he was lying low for a time while the law looked for him elsewhere.

She managed to control her agitation but the shock was still with her when they returned to the house. How could she get Frank alone so she could tell him? Or ought she to tell the sheriff?

Her opportunity came when Rita went to find Ben and tell him it was time to leave. Avon caught Frank's arm.

'I *must* speak to you alone! It is important!'

He looked quickly at her pale face and murmured: 'Come with me,' and led her into a small room furnished as an office. 'What is it? You have had a shock.'

'Yes, a dreadful shock! One of your men, that man who rode past us just now, is a train robber! He was with the gang who held up the train I was on when I came to Miles City! I recognised him by the stain on his cheek.'

'One of the train thieves?' Frank was staring at her. 'Dexter? He's been with me two months. You must be mistaken.'

'I am not. Oh, you must believe me, Frank. He came into the coach I was in and—and wanted to steal my watch . . . and then—' she paused, uncertain how much to tell him.

'But they said the men were masked, so how could you have seen his face?'

'There was a man with me; he knocked the thief down when he tried to take my watch and the mask slipped so I saw his face. I *know* I am right! I recognised him the moment I saw him. We must tell Sheriff Haskin at once, before the man gets away, Frank!'

Frank got up and began to stride to and fro, stroking his chin. Avon watched him in some surprise. She had expected him to take the matter at once to the sheriff.

Perhaps he still thought her mistaken.

'I haven't made a mistake, I *know* he was the train robber,' she insisted. 'What do you know of the man?'

'Nothing. You don't ask personal questions out here, it isn't polite—or safe. He's a good hand with horses, he's my corral boss and hasn't given any trouble so far.'

'He is a robber,' she said again. 'You must fetch the sheriff so I can tell him, Frank.'

He paused to stare out of the window, as if turning something over in his mind. She watched him, puzzled and impatient at his slowness in grasping the urgency of the situation.

'He may escape, Frank. Do fetch the sheriff.'

Frank transferred his gaze to her. He seemed to have made up his mind at last.

'Listen, Avon. I don't mean to tell Haskin anything, I can deal with this myself. I'll take Dexter, under guard, to Sweetwater and get the marshal there to lock him up.'

She looked at him in amazement. 'But why not get Sheriff Haskin to arrest him? He is here and—'

'I have my reasons for not using Haskin.' There was a note of sternness in his voice that arrested her attention. 'I can't tell you more; but I'm pretty certain my reasons are good ones. I'm going to ask you to trust me in this, to promise me not to say a word about recognising Dexter to anyone until he is safely behind bars in Sweetwater. Will you promise, Avon? Will you trust me to know what I am doing?'

She hesitated. 'I cannot imagine what reason you can possibly have for . . . Don't you trust the sheriff?'

For answer he came to her, putting his hands on her shoulders as he looked into her eyes.

'I can't say any more just now, Avon, I haven't enough to go on. But I beg you to trust me, and to say nothing of this until I tell you the man is in jail.'

Her eyes dropped before his intent gaze. 'Very well. But Frank,' she looked up quickly, 'if the man, Dexter, *did* know me, he will not stay here, he will escape.'

'I'm certain he didn't recognise you. He gave no sign.' He released her. 'Your people are ready to set off. I promise I will see to your train robber as soon as you have gone. Don't worry, I'll turn him in tomorrow and let the law take its course. By the way, did this other man in your coach see Dexter's face also?'

She thought quickly and decided the less said about 'the other man' the better. 'No.' She turned as her aunt called to her. 'I'm coming, Aunt Rita.'

She was silent on the way back, having plenty to occupy her thoughts. At first, the shock of seeing the train robber held her attention, but it slowly disappeared under the strange and disquieting remembrance of Frank's refusal to bring the sheriff into the matter. She glanced at the big man riding beside the buggy who was as silent as she, and whose thoughts were not pleasant ones judging by his expression. When they joined the main road, he bade them a brief goodbye and rode off.

Why had Frank distrusted Haskin? Did he know something discreditable about him or was it simply a personal dislike? Was it, perhaps, vanity on Frank's part that he wished to arrest the lawbreaker himself and turn him over to the law? The two men had always seemed friendly enough, but today something had undoubtedly upset Haskin's usual calm and, now she thought of it, he had appeared to avoid Frank and his manner had become somewhat reserved. The more she thought of it, the more she became convinced that Frank did not intend to let Haskin have the glory of capturing one of the infamous Blackface gang. There might be other reasons as well, but that was the strongest.

Rita, too, was silent. When she reached the farm, she said,

'You can come and unhook me, my arms don't work backwards.'

Avon helped to slip the dress off and hung it carefully in her aunt's press.

'It's a pretty colour enough,' Rita said, watching her. 'Minna always liked me to be in bright colours.'

Avon turned quickly. It was very seldom her aunt mentioned her dead daughter.

'I'm sure she is happy to know you have such a pretty new dress, Aunt Rita.'

Rita's sunken eyes fastened on her. 'How come she'll know? She's gone.'

'From this world, yes, but I am quite certain she knows about you and wants you to be happy.' Avon met the dark eyes steadily. 'I wouldn't want anyone I loved to waste their life sorrowing for me, it would make me terribly unhappy. We are not meant to be unhappy.'

Rita turned away slowly. 'Man was born to sorrow and sin.'

'Well, *I* believe he is meant to repent of his sins, and be happy.'

'You go and get out of your party dress and start supper for the men,' Rita said, but her voice had lost much of its sharpness. As Avon turned to go, she said: 'Wait a bit,' and pulled out a drawer from which she took a framed photograph. She held it out. 'Minna was just thirteen when it was done.'

Avon looked at the smiling girl whose dark curls and big, dark eyes could have been those of a younger, softer and gayer Rita, and her heart ached when she thought of what Rita and Ben had suffered in losing their only child.

'She is lovely,' she said gently. 'How proud you must have been to have a daughter like her.'

'She was taken from us!' 'There was no mistaking the pain in Rita's voice. 'The Lord gives—and takes away. Tell me why He had to take our Minna!'

'No one can tell that,' Avon said. 'We must believe in His purpose, and we shall know what it is one day.' As Rita opened the drawer, she added: 'Don't put Minna away, keep her where we can see her.'

Rita hesitated, then put the photograph on her dressing-table.

Avon slipped away and changed her dress and hurried to the kitchen to start heating up the stew that had been left ready. When her aunt came in, she was beating up flour, milk and eggs for the pancakes which Texas called 'flappers'.

Rita was quiet at supper. The geranium-petal colour had worn off and she was pale and looked tired but the harshness in her face was lacking. Ben glanced at her once or twice and then at Avon who was laughing at Texas's apprehension of her effect on the Two-Bar cowpunchers.

'Reckon we'll have our work cut out fighting 'em off,' he stated, spooning syrup over his plateful of pancakes. 'There'll be a track wore clean across the hills 'tween us and the Two-Bar. Ben had best get out that old deer gun of his.'

'I'll lend it to you, Tex,' Ben said.

'Me, I wouldn't know which end to use,' Texas declared, 'me not being handy with hardware at all.'

For some days Avon's thoughts continued to hover around the man she had seen at the Two-Bar, and she wondered greatly what had happened after she had left. Had Dexter resisted arrest? A man such as he would carry a gun and know how to use it. But he would be taken by surprise. Frank would have men to help him and perhaps even now, the man with the birthmark was behind bars in Sweetwater jail. No doubt she would be asked to give evidence against the robber. She wished Frank would come, or at least send some message. He must know how anxiously she waited for news.

She had promised not to speak of Dexter, but sometimes she wished she could tell Texas what had happened. She had learned to trust him, but of course she *had* promised Frank to say nothing.

And then Frank came riding over one afternoon. Avon was alone on the back porch and came running to the front of the house when she heard him call out.

'Frank, I've been longing to know what happened!

Did Dexter confess? Will the marshal want my evidence or—'

Frank raised a hand. 'Save your breath, Avon, I've bad news. Dexter must have recognised you. He had lit out by the time I went looking for him. Red told me he returned to the bunkhouse, collected his poke and went off without saying why, or waiting to get wages owing to him.'

She stared at him in dismay. 'He got away?'

'I'm afraid so. Dexter will be riding south and he'll avoid towns. The gang he's with will have a hide-out, probably in Wyoming. The Bighorn mountains could hide a hundred gangs—and stolen cattle. It could be Dexter was with the rustlers who had been plaguing us, he may have been the leader. Perhaps this will scare them away and if so, you have done us all a great service, Avon.'

'Oh, I hope so. But I wish he could have been caught, he will continue to rob and steal cattle.'

'Badmen like Dexter don't last long, either the law catches up with them or they shoot it out with another gang. You will keep your promise and say nothing?'

'You mean, you do not wish Sheriff Haskin to know about it?' she asked.

He nodded. 'I know I can trust you to keep it under your hat.'

She frowned in some perplexity. 'But if the law officer in Sweetwater knows—'

'He doesn't. There's no need for either he or Haskin to know anything just yet.'

She looked at him. 'Why do you not trust Haskin?'

He took a minute to answer her. 'I can't give my reasons yet, but I ask you to trust me, to understand that if I . . . mistrust Haskin, I have some grounds for it. You do trust me?'

'Yes, of course I do. But I am puzzled—' she stopped as Rita came out of the house with a bowl of washing.

'You can hang out this washing, Avon.' She gave Frank a sharp look. 'Business must be kind of slow at the Two-Bar when the boss finds time to pay social calls of an afternoon.'

Frank smiled at her. 'I'm on my way to Miles City, I have business there that will keep me away for a while. I called in passing to ask how you all were.'

'Well, Ben's well 'cept for a stiff back and you can see me and Avon ain't drooping yet. Get these clothes hung, Avon, 'fore the sun goes in.'

Frank looked up at the cloudless sky, smiled at Avon and took the hint.

Rita watched him ride off, her hands on her hips.

'Texas don't have to worry 'bout any Two-Bar boys coming visiting,' she said dryly, 'Frank Carline don't let no one ride his range.'

Harvesting was a busy time for all. Ben came in red-eyed with weariness at the end of the day and even Texas was showing some signs of strain. The hired men worked hard too, and ate voraciously the huge meals Rita and Avon cooked. Curly worked unwillingly and slipped off one night.

'Curly's a drifter,' Texas told Avon, 'he'll have one foot in his stirrup all his life, I reckon.'

Avon met Daisy in town and learned Frank was still away.

'Pheelie's been right-down scratchy lately,' she said, sharply for her. 'I had high words with her yesterday and we ain't speaking now.' She shrugged her shoulders. 'I reckon she'll get over it when she wants me to dress her hair for the barn dance. You heard of it, Avon? Two weeks come Saturday when harvest's over. It's real fun. Ma's ordered us dresses from Boston for it so we'll be right smart, but we won't be any prettier than you, Avon. I guess you look kind of elegant and ladylike no matter what you wear.'

Avon did not ask why it was necessary to order dresses from Boston for a local barn dance. Mrs Skellar considered herself the foremost lady in the district and her daughters to be leaders of fashion.

As Texas pulled up before the house when they returned from Sweetwater, Avon saw a small, brown-skinned woman in Indian clothes squatting by the verandah steps.

'That's Wana, a Sioux squaw,' Texas said. 'Comes round selling beadwork she's made. Right pretty some of it. You go take a look-see.'

Seeing Avon cross the yard, the squaw rose to her feet and pulled open a deerskin bag beside her. Her dark eyes rested on Avon intently before she said,

'You English woman?'

'Yes, I do come from England,' Avon said in some surprise.

The squaw grunted and began to pull out flat bands of bright beadwork, small mats with fringes and strings of gaudy beads.

'Pritty things,' she dangled the beads before Avon. 'Look nice. You buy?' She glanced at Texas who had joined them. 'Nice things for man too, pritty things for wife.'

'Seeing no woman's had the luck to cotch me yet, I ain't in need of dood-dangles,' Texas drawled. 'You got a deerskin 'baccy pouch, Wana?'

She took out a soft leather wallet and Avon listened, much amused, to the bargaining that went on between them until Texas had eventually bought the wallet and ambled away.

'I will buy this little fringed bag,' Avon said, picking it up. As she took her purse out of her pocket, the squaw, after a quick look around, touched her arm.

'He say I give you this. Is present from him. Take quick.'

Avon stared at the object Wana thrust at her, a wide bracelet worked in a pattern of blue lupins on a white ground.

'A present? From whom?'

'Man in hills,' Wana gestured towards the Indian Hills now hazy in midday heat. 'Man who hide . . . Ride up in sky. You take. He pay me.'

A quick excitement filled Avon as she stared at the charming little bracelet. So he had not left the hills. He was still riding the ridges by night, seeking . . . what? Surely he knew the law was hunting him? Why had he not fled to safer territory before this?

'You have seen him often? You know him? Where is your camp, Wana?'

'In hills.' The black eyes became blank. 'I see nothing. You pay two dollars for bag. I go.'

Avon gave her the money and said quickly: 'Say I am very pleased with the bracelet, tell him—'

'I tell nothing; I see nothing.' Wana gathered up her bag and walked away with the swift, shuffling Indian gait.

Avon stared after her, a dozen questions unanswered. Wana had seen Ken Grant, had spoken to him. Perhaps she knew where he hid. If she knew he was an outlaw— she had said 'man who hide'—she did not intend to give him away.

Rita called from the house and Avon hid the bracelet quickly and went indoors.

That night she lay awake for a long time, thinking of the man who must ride alone and by night, the man who was accused of murder, who had rescued her after the picnic, the man who had kissed her. He had sent her a gift. Had he asked the squaw to make a pattern of lupins, remembering she had gathered them that day? Probably she would never know. One day he would be caught, or he would disappear, and she would forget him. Or would she?

CHAPTER
EIGHT

Rita announced she wished to do some shopping in Sweetwater and would drive the buggy in and take Avon with her. The little town was looking dustier and drowsier than ever, but Avon was glad for a change from farm chores.

'I got business to do at the bank for Ben,' Rita said. 'You can visit with Kate Jonson and talk your head off 'bout folldidles for the barn dance. I'll pick you up.'

'Thank you, Aunt Rita.' Avon got down from the buggy and paused to look up at her aunt sitting straight as a sapling in her brown stuff dress and sunbonnet. 'You won't forget about—'

'Avon, you'll get me right riled if you say another word about curtains! I've said I'll buy the stuff and you can make 'em, though why in heaven's name clean sacking ain't good enough I'll never know!'

'It looks horrid, Aunt Rita—and Uncle Ben said you could buy material for new ones.'

'Ben's getting soft in his old age, he's better things to worry about than fancy curtains. Now quit staring me out of countenance, I'll buy it at Muller's and as sure as death he'll overcharge me. Don't you stray from Jonson's.'

Kate welcomed her exuberantly and they sat down together over a cup of coffee and a buttered slice of the warm, sweet-smelling bread Mrs Jonson had taken from the oven.

'Now Avon, I've the greatest idea for you, if your aunt allows it.' Kate's eyes sparkled as she stared at Avon across the scrubbed pine table. 'My Aunt Sukey over

Freeland way's asked me to visit four days and Ma says she can spare me since the travelling preacher won't be coming just yet awhile.'

'I am so glad you will have a little holiday, Kate.'

'Well it's my idea you have a holiday too, Avon, and come with me. Aunt Sukey said for me to bring a friend if I cared. She's real nice, not like—' she broke off, her cheeks tinged with pink. 'The farm is a big one and Uncle Jake keeps it good. Cousin Tom—he's their only son—is fifteen and a real tease, but I guess he'll take a fall when he sees you. Will your folks let you come?'

'Why Kate, it sounds delightful and I would love to come, but I am not sure if . . . I will ask my aunt when she comes.'

'Best let Ma talk to her,' Kate said shrewdly. 'Ma and your aunt used to meet before Minna died.'

'*Would* you ask her, Mrs Jonson?' Avon looked up at the tall, fresh-faced woman stacking the washed bread pans.

'Why sure I will, Avon. It's time Rita took thought for you a mite more. I reckon young girls ought to be let off the hook sometimes.'

'Aunt Rita is kind to me,' Avon said quickly. 'I don't have to work hard.'

'Well I'm pleased to know it. Will you be going to the barn dance at the end of harvest? It's a real fine evening for young and old.'

'I hope so.'

Rita arrived and was taken into the best parlour by Mrs Jonson. When it was time to leave, Avon unhitched the horse, climbed into the buggy and took up the reins—Texas had taught her to drive—and they set off. Her aunt waited until they had left the town before remarking,

'So you're invited to stay up at the Olsson's farm with Kate?'

'It was very kind of Kate to suggest it and I *would* like

to go if you and Uncle Ben can spare me. I know it is a busy time—'

'No busier than other years. You can go. Sukey Olsson's a decent woman—and you'll find her curtains ain't made from flour sacks.'

'Oh, did you get material?'

'I did, and you can get busy sewing the minute we get home. Kate's uncle is driving her to the farm on Friday and will call for you.'

'How good of him.' Avon turned a glowing face to Rita. 'It is very kind of you to allow me to go.'

There was a short silence before Rita said reflectively: 'Well, I reckon I don't often get accused of kindness.'

Avon sang softly to herself as she sewed the printed cotton curtains for her aunt's and her own bedroom and—although Rita protested—for the kitchen. Her heart was light at the thought of a visit away with Kate. She determined to forget the escape of the train robber and her uneasiness over what Frank had hinted about Sheriff Haskin and banish, if she could, her haunting awareness of Ken Grant still riding the high bluffs of the Indian Hills. She wondered if the squaw had seen him again and conveyed her thanks for the gift he had sent. It had been a risky thing to do. There was a price on his head that could tempt the squaw to denounce him, and yet she had refused to speak of him and pretended to know nothing.

The curtains were finished by Friday and Ben nodded approvingly when he saw the result of her work and Texas suggested she should fix a fancy shirt for him out of material left over, so he could shine at the barn dance.

'Guess you'll miss the dance now you're taking time off after harvest,' Ben remarked.

Avon looked up. 'Are you going away, Texas?'

He shrugged as he spooned sugar into his coffee. 'Guess my feet get a mite itchy at times. I'll maybe mosey south for a spell and see some of my pals.'

'But you will come back?' she asked anxiously.

'Why for sure, Avon, you don't get rid of me that easy. Your aunt's cooking is mighty tempting, and now we're all spragged up with new curtains . . .'

Ben got up from the breakfast table. 'You all ready for your visit to the Olsson's, Avon?'

'Yes, Uncle Ben. My case is packed. Why! Here they come!'

She jumped up and hastened to get her hat, bag and dust coat. Mr Olsson, a lean, blond man, was talking to Ben from his seat on the spring wagon when she came out of the house. After bidding her aunt and uncle goodbye, she got into the wagon beside Kate.

There was a pleasant coolness in the air now the sun was losing some of its midsummer fierceness. The land was looking dry and the bunch grass had a yellow tinge. The Olsson farm lay to the west, not far from the foothills of the mountain range. The drive was a long one but Avon enjoyed it and the unaccustomed sense of freedom. She and Kate chatted happily about neighbours and the coming dance.

'The Skellars pretend they don't take much note of it,' Kate said, 'it being kind of rough and unrefined to their ideas. But Pheelie and Daisy have new dresses, and Mrs Skellar will out-smart the other wives, just as sure as death.'

Avon thought of something. 'Is Frank Carline back?'

'I guess not, or Pheelie'd be looking less sour.' Kate glanced shrewdly at Avon. 'She sure looked mean at you on the picnic. I've had a notion maybe she—'

'Don't let's discuss it,' Avon said quickly. 'I expect something had upset her that day.'

'It sure had—and I reckon I know what it was. Howsomever, she'll not catch Frank that way, turning green when he looks at another girl.'

The Olsson farmhouse was a long and rambling building. The original one-storey house had been added to haphazardly over the years. The main bedrooms lay on the south side but Avon's little bedroom, which had once been a storeroom, was next the kitchen, away from the rest of the house, and looked across a field to a small corral and some farm buildings.

Mrs Olsson greeted her warmly and had a meal ready. Tom, Kate's young cousin, stared admiringly at Avon and turned pink whenever she spoke to him.

During the meal, Mr Olsson reminded his wife that he and Tom were hunting deer in the hills the next day.

'Mebbe we'll get some game too,' he said. 'Get the girls to help set us up some food before we go, we'll not be back before dark.'

'I'd best get it ready tonight,' his wife said, 'since you'll be starting at sun up.'

Avon and Kate helped wash dishes and then cut meat and bread for the hunters. Avon was pleasantly tired when she went to bed and slept soundly until Kate came to wake her next morning. The two girls helped with housework and feeding stock and then went riding on two of the farm ponies. As she rode, Avon's eyes turned often to the harsh hills that rose so abruptly in the west. The foothills were green and slashed with lush valleys and narrow ravines, but above the timber-line rose bare rock, seamed and pocketed with gullies, looking bleak and chill. She thought of the time she had seen the silent horseman standing on a bluff keeping watch—for pursuers?

'Uncle knows those hills well,' Kate told Avon as they turned their ponies homeward. 'There's plenty of game there, and fish in the streams, only it ain't easy to fish, the streams being cut deep in the rock.'

'Does Mr Olsson ever meet any—any people there?'

'Guess not, only perhaps a few Indians. The Sioux are plainspeople, not many live in the hills.'

Avon rode back in silence, only half hearing Kate's chatter. The strange awareness of the man they called the sky rider was stronger than ever now she was near his hiding place—if he *was* still there, of course, she reminded herself quickly.

Supper was over and cleared away and night had
fallen before Avon heard the beat of horses's hooves and
saw Mrs Olsson turn her head and say: 'That's Pa. Who's
with him?'

Kate jumped up as a man shouted and the three
women hurried onto the verandah. Mrs Olsson called
out,

'Who've you got there, Pa? Did something happen?'

From the group of dimly seen horsemen, her husband
shouted,

'Sure did, Ma! Hank and Bill Garson met up with us
and we've caught a man that's wanted by the law!'

'Well for goodness' sake!' Mrs Olsson peered out at
the men now dismounting. 'I thought you went hunting
deer.'

'We cotched more'n deer, Ma!' Tom's voice, shrill
with triumph, rang out. 'There's a reward on him! I've
seen a poster of him!'

Avon caught at the verandah rail to steady herself as
her heart began to race crazily. There was only one man
they could have captured! With wide eyes she watched
the men dismount and in the light streaming from the
open door she saw a tall man being pulled down from his
horse, a man with his hands tied behind him . . . Ken
Grant!

Sound and sight blurred for a moment. She heard
men's voices; Jake's: 'I'll put him in the side shed, there
ain't no window and the lock's good and strong. Ma,
fetch a pitcher of water and cut bread, I don't aim to
starve any man no matter what he's done.' A strange
voice said: 'You're sure he'll stay there, Jake? He broke
jail in Laramie.' Another voice broke in. 'Hank and me
will ride over tomorrow early and we'll get him to
Sweetwater. Reckon Sheriff Haskin's still there. He's
been looking for this gent awhiles.'

'Get the key of the shed, Ma,' Jake Olsson ordered. 'It
hangs in the kitchen. And you can rustle up some coffee
for us.'

Avon forced herself to move away from the verandah rail.

'I'll make coffee,' she said through stiff lips, and went into the kitchen where Mrs Olsson was cutting bread, her face troubled.

'I guess he got what was coming to him,' she said. 'He killed a man and broke jail. But I don't like the notion we're helping to hang a man, Avon.'

'Perhaps he will be proved innocent.'

Mrs Olsson brushed back a lock of hair. 'Innocent men have been hanged before this,' she said and started to bail water from a pail into a pitcher.

Avon set the kettle to boil. She had the feeling that none of this was happening. It was almost as if she were a spectator watching a play. It was not real. It was some nightmare happening and she would soon wake up and thank God she had been dreaming.

She had seen Grant only for a moment as he was dragged from his horse. His dark hair had fallen across his forehead and his eyes, those cool, deeply blue eyes she remembered so well, had met hers without a sign of recognition. Then he had been hustled away by Jake and the two men who must be the Garson brothers. Tom had started to follow but had been curtly ordered by Jake to look to the horses.

Kate's eyes were round with excitement.

'Well to goodness! If that ain't something, catching a murderer that's been roaming loose all this while!'

'Cut bacon and hot up the biscuits left from supper, girls,' Mrs Olsson ordered. 'The men will be hungry.'

Avon set to work, a mounting horror growing as she realised this was no dream. How had Ken Grant been caught after so long evading capture? He knew the hills better than most; the sheriff had said he had chosen them because he knew their torturous canyons and valleys, and caves hollowed by the years into hiding places where a man might lie hidden or defend himself against attack. The Garson boys were tough-looking youngsters with the early maturity Western life brought to men in their tanned faces. Her impatience was at breaking point by the time the men returned and sat down to the meal.

'How did you get Grant?' Kate asked.

Hank Garson grinned at her. 'Bill went higher than usual and saw smoke. He sneaked down and saw Grant making camp. Grant looked kind of beat and Bill reckoned he'd sleep heavy. He fetched up your uncle and Tom and me and we waited till Bill had indianed up on Grant and got the jump on him. Grant didn't get time to get his gun out and we closed in. He didn't give no trouble, I guess he knew he was for a quick trial and a necktie party!' He guffawed and returned to his bacon and eggs.

Mrs Olsson touched Avon's arm. 'You look tuckered out, child. Go to your bed.'

Avon was thankful to obey. In her room, she pulled aside the curtain and looked out. The moon was a thin crescent in a purple sky and racing scud veiled the stars. She could not see the shed where Ken Grant lay awaiting his journey to Sweetwater and the sheriff tomorrow. There would be no breaking out of the shed, Jake Olsson had said it was sturdily built. She pulled the curtains across, shutting out the night, but not her fears.

She got into bed but knew sleep was far away and lay listening to the sounds of the household settling down to sleep. The Garsons had ridden off and the clatter of dishes was stilled. The last door had been shut and now the wind was making itself heard, flapping a loose fence board, whining around corners and making the windbreak of willows creak drearily.

An owl hooted, recalling her vigil in the valley, and she shivered and sat up. Her mouth was dry and she decided to get a drink of water and, slipping on her wrap, she lit her candle and crept softly into the kitchen. As she reached for the ladle beside the water pail she saw something that drove all thought of thirst out of her mind. On a nail by the pail hung a key and beside it hung a gun-belt she recognised as belonging to Ken.

She stood staring at it, transfixed by the tumult of thought bursting in upon her! The key meant freedom for the man in the shed who might yet take part in a 'necktie party'. She felt a draught chill her bare feet and turned to see the kitchen window had been left slightly open.

Moved by something stronger than her own will and making her blind to the risk she ran, her hand went up to unhook the key and gun-belt. Shielding the candle flame with one hand, she stood listening intently. A passage-way and a storeroom separated her from the other rooms; it was unlikely any noise would be heard above the rising wind. Her heart thudded so fiercely that for a second she felt faint. Then, suddenly, she felt courage flow through her and blew out the candle and turned to the window.

At first the blackness blinded her, then as she leant out she began to discern objects in the faint light. She slid the window open and sat on the ledge before letting herself down gently until her feet touched the ground. It felt hard and dry and her mind registered the fact that it would take no footprints.

She waited, listening intently and staring around. Then catching her wrap around her as the wind pulled at it, she crossed the rough grass to the track leading to the shed.

The key was stiff in the lock but she managed to turn it at last. As the door swung open, she leant forward and whispered: 'Ken?'

She felt him beside her before she could see him, a dark shape tall above her.

'Avon! How in heaven—'

'Oh hush! Here is your belt and gun. Are your hands still tied?'

'No.' He took the belt and buckled it swiftly about his waist. 'You must get back before you're missed. I know

Darkie is in the corral. Where are the saddles kept?'

'In the barn, it isn't locked. You must get away at once!'

'Avon,' his voice deepened, 'why did you do it?'

'I—I was afraid of what might happen . . . Oh please, go *now*!'

For answer he picked her up and she found herself being carried back to the house. She struggled and whispered.

'Let me go! Someone may come! It isn't safe for you to stay!'

He helped her to slip in the window. Then he stooped and came up with some earth in his hand which he smeared on the sill.

'Take this dirt,' he thrust it into her hand, 'and drop a little on the floor to look like someone's got in by the window and lifted the key and belt. I'll trample grass under the window, the ground's too hard for any prints.'

'Very well,' she said breathlessly.

'This is the second time you've saved me from something mighty unpleasant.' She could not see his face, only his tall figure against the faint light. 'First time I knew I had a guardian angel. Does this mean you don't think I'm a killer?'

She stared up at him, her hands clasped to her breast.

'No,' suddenly she knew she had never truly believed it. 'No, I do not. There was some mistake . . . it was an accident, or . . . How did it happen?'

'That's what I'm setting out to find,' he said harshly, 'that, and the man whose shot killed Jones—and who framed me. Avon,' he bent towards her. 'I reckon I can't thank you . . . I haven't the words for it.'

'I don't want them,' she whispered. 'Please, *please* go *now*. And—and good luck go with you!'

'You called me by name. Say it again.'

'Ken', she said softly, and moved back into the shadows. She waited, straining her ears, her taut nerves near breaking point. She heard a faint whistle and a

horse whicker and knew Darkie had answered the signal
from the corral. Then silence. He would be saddling up
the big black horse. A soft jingle of harness; hoofbeats
slow and cautious, then silence. The wind was dropping
and cloud had returned. Darkness would be his friend.

She scattered the grains of earth he had given her on
the floor and, taking her candle, crept back to her room.

Reaction came. She had released a man the law called
a murderer! She herself was a lawbreaker now and
perhaps tomorrow would bring discovery and retribu-
tion! She had pitted her will against the men who
claimed to have proof of Ken's guilt and who would try
him and hang him.

'But he isn't a criminal,' she thought. 'He didn't kill.
He may have done other things—but I do not believe he
is a killer. I do not care if they discover what I have done!
I am glad! Ken is free, and I pray he can prove his
innocence one day!'

Rain came, a soft patter on her window at first, then a
steady drumming on the roof and she nestled into her
pillows with a sigh of relief. Rain would obliterate any
tell-tale tracks left by Darkie. Ken was safe for the time
being—and she had saved him. He would not be caught
the same way again, his capture would make him more
careful. But he would stay in the hills, riding the ridges at
night, a lone, grim figure searching for the truth that
would prove him innocent, truth which he suspected was
hidden in the territory. And the man who had framed
him, was he too hiding deep in those rugged hills?

The night brought no answer.

CHAPTER
NINE

'Come wake, Avon,' Kate cried, bursting into Avon's room. 'Mercy on us, such happenings! Uncle's gone to feed his prisoner and found he's taken off like he was never there!'

Avon sat up, brushing her tangled curls out of her eyes. 'What? I don't understand, Kate. What has happened?'

'Ain't I telling you? Ken Grant, the man Uncle and the Garsons brought in last night, is clean gone and disappeared! Someone's come and loosed him 'cause the key's in the door and there's signs, Uncle says, that someone's got into the kitchen. Aunt Sukey forgot to shut the window last night.'

'But who could have done it?' Tense and with quickened heartbeat, Avon awaited the answer.

'Uncle says Grant must of had a pal who followed him and saw where he was put and let him out. Grant's horse is gone and there's no tracks 'cause of the rain. Uncle's asking for you.'

Avon caught her breath. 'Me?'

'Yes, he wants to know if you heard anything last night, you being nearest the kitchen.'

'I—I'll come as soon as I've dressed.'

She waited until Kate had left before getting out of bed, remembering her feet were dirty from last night and might cause comment. She dressed hastily and went into the kitchen where Olsson sat at a table while his wife cooked breakfast. Tom was wandering about restlessly, looking at the empty pegs where the key and gun-belt had hung, and then going to stare out of the window. He turned as Avon entered.

'Great jiminy, Avon, Grant's got away! Someone snuck, in last night an'—'

'Hush up,' his father said. 'Avon, did you hear any sounds last night? I expect Kate's told you we're missing a prisoner.'

'Yes, she did.' Avon sank into a chair and helped herself to a cup of coffee, feeling she needed it. She must appear astonished, shocked—and innocent. 'I'm afraid the wind was making too much noise for me to hear anything, Mr Olsson. I was very sleepy and I don't remember waking at any time.'

'She's right,' Mrs Olsson said, putting her husband's plate of pork and beans before him. 'The wind sure raised a rumpus around the house. I just can't figure out how someone followed the men and saw where Grant was put.'

'What makes you think it was one of his friends?' Avon asked.

'Who else? There was dirt on the sill and on the floor and the grass trampled outside the window. Rain's washed out any signs of which way they went.'

'Well I'm darn well *glad*!' Tom said unexpectedly. 'Grant's broken jail twice, it looks as if he ain't *meant* to hang.' He shook his head. 'Mebbe he didn't kill that fellow after all.'

'Mistakes can happen in a bar fight,' his father allowed him, 'but the barman swears he saw Grant fire at the man and that's enough to hang him.' He looked up. 'That'll be Hank and his brother, I sent over for them.'

Avon took her cup of coffee out onto the back porch. The men's excited voices reached her as she sat sipping her coffee, her eyes following the green foothills up to the stands of yellow pine and further, to the harsh rocky face of the Indian Hills. She was safe! No one suspected her! Knowing she was from England and still new to the West, who would think she would risk being found out in helping a wanted man to escape? No one knew she had ever met Grant—except Texas. She wondered suddenly if Texas would guess anything of last night's work. As he had once told her, his guesses had a way of turning out right. But Texas would never give her away, and she had a sudden longing to see his brown, seamed face and bright, observant eyes and hear his lazy drawl.

Kate came out to join her, full of excitement. The Garson boys were 'plenty sore', she said, at Grant's escape and were all for pursuing him and his pal, a proposal they abandoned when Olsson pointed out they had no notion in which direction the men had gone.

'Grant won't stay in these parts now,' Hank was saying gloomily when Avon and Kate returned to the kitchen, 'I reckon it's farewell to that reward.' His glance went to Kate who coloured up and dropped her eyes. 'I'd best ride into Sweetwater and give Haskin the story so's he can pass word Grant's still on the loose.' He got up. 'Any message for your folks, Kate? I can drop by if you want.'

'Why I guess so, Hank. You tell her Avon and me's having a fine visit . . .' They passed out onto the front steps. Avon's eyes followed them. She had not missed Kate's blush or the look in Hank's eyes and guessed the source of some of Kate's pleasure in her visit.

The next days passed quietly. There was still talk about Grant's escape, but no more speculation about it. Some pal of Grant's had seen his capture, followed and discovered where he was imprisoned and, finding the kitchen window open, got the key and released him. The open question was who the pal might be, the general opinion being that Grant had joined another outlaw, or a gang, hiding in the hills.

'Well there ain't ever been *two* sky riders,' Tom declared. 'I reckon Grant's pal was too scared to show himself ever. Grant sure had guts,' he ended admiringly.

Mr Olsson drove Avon home after she had thanked his wife warmly for having her to stay.

Mrs Olsson had assured her she was very welcome to come with Kate any time she wished.

'You've been good for Kate,' she said as she stood watching her niece get into the wagon, 'she ain't near so rough mannered as she was. You've got pretty, gentle ways, Avon, and Kate admires you mightily.'

Both girls were somewhat silent on the drive. Avon was living again the experience of the night she rescued Ken Grant, and Kate, she suspected, was wrapped in rosy dreams of Hank and the coming dance.

Olsson stayed long enough at the farm to tell Ben and Rita the news. When he had gone, Ben remarked to Avon,

'You got more than you expected at the Olsson farm, I guess. Did you see the man?'

'Just a glimpse of him,' she admitted. 'It was night when they brought him in.'

'Mighty careless of Sukey to leave a window open and the key in sight,' Rita remarked.

'I expect she forgot it in all the fuss and excitement,' Avon said. 'I don't think she was very upset when he escaped, she said she didn't like to think they were helping to get a man hanged.'

'Sukey Olsson was always kind of soft,' Rita said. 'But I guess I might feel like that myself, maybe.'

Avon found Texas had delayed leaving to see her. Next morning he came to where she was hanging out the wash and took his seat on the tree stump and began to roll a cigarette.

'Heered you ran into a mite of excitement at Olsson's,' he remarked.

'Indeed I did,' Avon left the washing to sit beside him. 'I expect you have heard all about it.'

Texas drew on his smoke thoughtfully. 'Mebbe . . . and mebbe not. Seems funny no one knowed he had a pal moseying around.'

'Perhaps he had just joined Grant,' she suggested quickly and decided to change the conversation. 'Where are you making for, Texas?'

'Me, I'm taking the south trail.'

'I think you once said something about Laramie.'

'Yep. Used to know that town mighty well once.' He chuckled. 'I reckon there's some bar-rooms ain't forgot me yet.'

'Well at least you never did any shooting since you can't use a gun.'

'Sure. But I got kind of skittish when I was drinking and I had the idea I was an opery singer and there was hombres as sometimes objected. One travelling gent asked me to quit my death rattle and there was quite a ruckus.' He shook his head meditatively. 'I sure didn't ought to have hit him so hard, him being bigger than me.'

Avon laughed and squeezed his arm. 'Well, keep out of trouble this time, please—and don't be operatic! I shall miss you. Come back soon.'

'Sure I will. Ben's hired a hand for a month and I'll be back by then. An' you keep yourself out of trouble, Avon.' His eyes were a little too penetrating for her liking. 'It's my guess you can act a mite too quick sometimes.'

'Don't all women?' she asked lightly, and rose to finish hanging out the wash. Texas could not know she had been the 'pal' who had released Ken—or could he?

The harvest was almost in. Avon went with her aunt to a neighbour's corn-husking bee where the green husks were gathered to be dried and used for filling mattresses, a proceeding which revealed to Avon why her bed was so unlike her English one. She met other girls, but not the Skellars, and the talk was all of the coming dance. It was to be held in a large barn and everyone was expected to bring something for the supper. Rita had announced firmly that she was too busy to waste time on such foolishness, but she had promised to make two pumpkin pies and a batch of malasses cookies for Avon to take. The Mullers were bringing Kate and her mother and would call for Avon.

Avon was grateful for anything that would take her

mind away from her experience at the Olsson farm. Against her will, she found her thoughts returning to that night and to speculation on where Ken was now and if he was any nearer to discovering who had fired the fatal shot and why a witness had sworn he was the culprit. Had the barman been bribed? Could he have left Laramie and be somewhere in this part of the territory and had Ken trailed him and was waiting to force the truth from him?

From her uncle she learned more cattle were being stolen and the hunt for the rustlers was to be intensified although, to the ranchers' anger, Sheriff Haskin was slow to agree and indeed appeared to be holding up proceedings.

'I don't know what he is at,' Ben grumbled. 'It will be a case of vigilantes if the law doesn't take it up. There was an outbreak of crime some years ago, same as now, and the vigilantes put a stop to it. There's organised crime here, not just a band of badmen cutting up. A kid who got in the way of a bank raid in the city last week was killed. I was talking to Carline about it.'

Avon looked up from the bread dough she was kneading. 'Then he is back?'

'Yes. Now you girls can fight over who's going to dance with him.' He nodded at her floury hands. 'You have learned quickly to make good bread, Avon.'

'Aunt Rita taught me. She has taught me many useful things.'

'She likes doing it,' Ben said. 'I don't say she made you welcome at first, Avon, but it's different now. She missed you when you visited the Olssons, and she was truly scared that time you were left in the hills alone.'

Avon drew in a quick breath. '*Was* she? I—I'm glad she does not resent me now, Uncle Ben.'

He nodded as he rose. 'I'm glad too. She has Minna's photograph out and talks about her now, I never thought she would. That was your doing and I'm grateful.'

Avon continued her kneading with a heart suddenly

lightened. Rita no longer snapped at her and her eyes were not so cold and her words not so abrasive. It was good to know from her uncle that she was no longer a thorn in her aunt's side.

She had made her choice of dress for the dance, a white muslin trimmed with ruchings of leaf-green ribbon. The tight elbow sleeves ended in ruffles and the draped skirt showed off her slender figure. It was one of the English dresses she had brought with her.

Rita eyed it approvingly. 'It's real pretty and not too dressy. You'll need a shawl; come dark it'll be chill. There's a wool lace shawl Minna used to wear, you can have it.'

The shawl was charming and Avon thanked her aunt warmly for letting her have it and some of the warmth was reflected in Rita's dark eyes as she said,

'You'll outshine those Skellar girls. I reckon Pheelie will have a conniption fit when she sees you.' There was no mistaking the satisfaction in her words. 'Pheelie'll be in sky-blue and Daisy in yellow.'

'How did you discover that, Aunt Rita?'

'Huh! Tumbleweed ain't the only thing that rolls around. Don't let Frank Carline tie you up for too many dances, Avon.'

'I don't suppose he'll want to.'

'Quit looking kitten-soft. He'll get his rope around you in two shakes if you don't watch him.'

'Don't you like Frank?'

Rita took a minute before replying. 'I reckon there's nothing to dislike in him 'cept he's too good-looking and knows it, and he has too much money to throw about.'

'That isn't a crime,' Avon said, laughing. 'Does Sheriff Haskin condescend to go to a barn dance?'

'Never knowed him to, but it's my guess you'll see him there.' Rita flicked a glance at Avon as she folded the ironing. 'Reckon a man can be foolish no matter what his age.'

On the day of the dance, Avon watched the sky

anxiously. Rain would not prevent the dance from being held but it would spoil some of the pleasure of being able to spread the supper on trestle tables under the big cottonwoods and would certainly spoil the hopes of the young cowpunchers busy 'getting theirselves into their low-neck clothes' as Texas put it, who hoped for a stroll in the dark with their partners between dances.

However the threatening clouds moved away and all promised well.

As the Muller wagon drove off, Avon turned to see Ben and Rita standing on the steps, waving to her, and rush of loving happiness brought a mist to her eyes as she waved back. They were her family, their home was her home. She loved them! Why had she not realised it before! Her uncle, taciturn and grave, but aware of her and pleased she had come to live at the farm, and her aunt who had so resented her and who had, she hoped, come to accept her and perhaps even to grow fond of her. Impulsively she said to Kate sitting beside her,

'They have been so good to me. Probably they did not truly want me, but they gave me a home when my father and step-mother refused to. I am happy with them and I hope I can make them happy.'

'You sure have made your aunt look more like she used to,' Kate's mother remarked from behind her. 'Rita was a frozen woman after Minna died and you've thawed her out, Avon. Ben will love you for that, if for nothing else.'

'And there's plenty else,' Kate declared, tucking her hand under Avon's arm. 'Are you excited about the dance, Avon?'

'Oh yes—even though I realise Hank Garson won't ask *me* to dance.' Avon said mischievously.

Kate giggled happily. 'Well Frank Carline won't take long to lead you out on the floor, Avon Meredith.'

The big barn had been emptied of all but benches along the sides, and there was a roped-off section at one end where the band—two fiddles, a concertina and a banjo—were to perform. The walls were hung with bunting and a highly coloured print of the President was encircled with sprays of evergreens. The floor had been sprinkled with cornstarch which, when pounded in by the dancer's feet, was supposed to make it smooth. Wagons, buggies and horses were coming from all directions and greetings filled the cool evening air.

'For mercy's sake,' Kate whispered, 'see the Skellars' new surrey! I heard Mrs Skellar had ordered it. It sure looks swell.'

It was an elegant affair with a fixed roof ornamented with a deep silk fringe, and it had fenders to prevent mud or dust reaching passengers. Gleaming brass lamps added the last touch of grandeur and there was an audible indrawing of breath as it drove up.

'If Mame Skellar don't take heed her carriage'll outshine her in elegance,' Mrs Jonson observed caustically. 'Help me down, Kate, I ain't used to so many petticoats.'

The musicians were tuning up as they approached the barn. An outhouse had been made into a ladies' cloakroom and a babble of feminine voices broke over Avon and Kate as they pushed their way in. When they emerged, women were spreading white cloths on the long trestle tables while men erected the barrels of beer necessary to replace moisture lost by the masculine dancers during the evening. Stronger drink was discreetly hidden behind the barn. The ladies were to be regaled with fruit cup.

A wave of happy excitement ran through Avon as she watched the lively scene. This was nothing like the balls she had attended in England. Here, the entertainment was simpler, rougher, cruder and more unrestrainedly gay. She had a fleeting vision of what some of her English friends would think if they were set down in the midst of all this and she could not help smiling.

'You are looking happy,' Frank's voice made her start, 'and very beautiful. No, please don't scold me, I had to say it because it is true. You are like a lovely flower.'

She regarded him thoughtfully, her head tilted a little to one side.

'If you start the evening with compliments,' she said demurely but with laughter lurking in her grey eyes, 'you will have none left by the end.'

'But I do not pay compliments,' he murmured, coming closer, 'I tell the truth, and it is never too early to do that.'

She drew back slightly. 'Did you have a pleasant visit away?'

He shrugged. 'Business trips are always boring, although necessary, and this time I was very impatient to return.' His eyes, bent on hers, told her why, but she chose to ignore it. She was conscious of interested glances turned on them as they stood talking. Frank was looking extraordinarily handsome in his dark suit, white shirt and brocaded waistcoat. His dark hair was smooth —but not by the application of the bear grease so beloved of the cowpunchers when they attended social events.

She was about to speak when she saw the Skellar family coming towards them. Mrs Skellar was tightly encased in gold satin and Pheelie's pale blue gown enhanced her white-and-gold beauty. Daisy was in pale yellow taffeta and Avon thought she looked uneasy.

Frank was murmuring in her ear: 'Am I allowed the honour of the first dance with you, Avon?'

'I—I am afraid I am engaged for the first dance,' she said quickly.

'Then the second?' he pleaded eagerly and she agreed before moving away. She had seen Pheelie's face and felt disturbed. There was no doubt in her mind that the girl was in love with Frank, and that Frank had flirted with her before his interest moved elsewhere and, despite her suspicions of the picnic incident, she could not help feeling sorry for the pain Pheelie must feel when she faced the truth.

She realised she must get herself a partner somehow since she had pretended to be engaged. She looked around and saw young Ted Skellar staring at her and smiled at him, a smile that brought him racing to her side.

'Why, hello, Miss Avon. Daisy and me haven't been over to see you 'cause Ma's been flustering everyone 'bout dresses and such for the dance. You sure do look nice. You going in to dance?'

'I hope so, if I'm asked, Ted.'

His eyes widened and his freckles lost themselves in a wave of scarlet.

'You mean . . . If I asked you . . . The very *first* dance?'

'The very first dance, Ted. Let us go in, I think they are beginning.'

They joined a group for a square dance as the fiddles struck up. Ted, bursting with pride, pranced like a young cockerel, swung Avon off her feet, and executed weird and wonderful steps of his own invention. Avon saw Frank enter with Pheelie on his arm. She hoped she had not hurt his feelings, but surely he must know it would have been unwise for him to have danced the opening dance with anyone but Pheelie. He had known the family for so long, and enjoyed their hospitality so often that it would have been an ungracious thing to do.

The barn soon became hot in spite of the open windows. Perspiring young cowpunchers and farm hands twisted and turned, whirled partners, changed hands and thumped the floor to the rhythm of the squealing fiddles until forced to retire in the direction of the beer barrels. Their partners retired to pin up torn flounces, restore order to hair arrangements and rub scarlet cheeks with powdered starch.

Avon was soon besieged with shy but persistent partners. She danced with Frank more than once, and with

Bill Garson who was too shy to make conversation for which she was grateful as she did not wish to discuss the incident at the Olsson farm.

The heat began to make her feel slightly dizzy so she slipped away to walk for a little in the shadow of the trees now that a cool breeze had sprung up. Not wishing to be sought by eager partners, she strolled through the thick belt of trees and found herself in a narrow valley holding a small creek. She wandered along its banks, grateful for the quiet and the cool air on her hot skin.

She heard a horse's hoof-beat behind her but did not turn. A late-comer to the dance, no doubt. Suddenly the rider was beside her and as she looked up, startled, he bent down, caught her up and swung her up before him on his saddle!

The horse sprang forward in response to a spur and Avon gasped, her head whirling as she clung, to prevent herself falling, to the man who had abducted her.

The horse struck across the creek, up the opposite bank and down into a stretch of pinewood where the man pulled his mount up.

'I'm sorry if I scared you—but I had to speak to you. I couldn't believe my luck when I saw you walking alone along the creek.'

She looked up at him then, at the lean, unshaven chin, haggard eyes and grimly set mouth and jaw and her anger died.

'What are you doing here, Ken? Someone will surely see you! How could you be so rash! I heard the sheriff might be coming; if he should see you . . .'

'He won't. I guessed you would be at the dance and I took the chance of meeting you. No one would notice a horseman riding this way tonight. Tell me, Avon, is Carline here tonight?'

'Yes, he has been away for a time but he is back . . . Oh, I must tell you: that train robber, the one you hit, was working for Frank! I saw him when I visited the Two-Bar ranch.'

'One of Carline's men?' Ken demanded sharply. 'Did he know you?'

'I did not think so, but he must have because when Frank went to arrest him he had disappeared. I—I wanted Frank to tell Sheriff Haskin who was there but . . . Well he seemed reluctant, almost as if—as if he did not trust Haskin.'

'Didn't trust Haskin?' Ken raised his head and stared into the shadows. 'Now that's . . . interesting.'

'Have you found out anything about why you were accused of murder?' she asked eagerly.

'Not yet,' he said slowly, 'but it was a frame-up all right. Someone wanted young Jones out of the way, and pinned the killing on me. He was a stranger to the town and had got talking once the whiskey loosened his tongue. He got fresh with me and I roughed him up a bit—and that told against me, I reckon.'

'The bar-tender?'

'He told his story mighty slick. He was new to the town also, half Mexican. I've learned he owns the saloon now.'

'Then he was bribed!' she cried. 'I thought that might be so. He was given money enough to buy the saloon.'

'It won't be easy to prove.' His arm tightened around her as he looked down at her lying against his breast. 'Avon, *you* know I'm not a killer, or a rustler. That's meant a whole heap to me, it's helped me to fight on.'

'Oh, I'm glad! But must you stay in the Indian Hills now that it is known you are there?'

'Yes.' She felt his body tighten. 'There are things I don't understand in those hills—and I mean to find out. I'm taking you back before you're missed.' He swung the big black horse around.

She did not speak until they had recrossed the creek and come up to the belt of cottonwoods where he dismounted and swung her to the ground. Then she said, a little breathlessly,

'I haven't yet thanked you for the bracelet Wana

brought. It is charming. Look,' she held out her arm, 'I am wearing it.'

His hand closed on her wrist. 'You knocked up that gun in the train,' he said slowly, 'and didn't give me away after. You weren't scared when I found you in the valley. And you took a hell of a risk to get me out of Olsson's shed. You're my girl, Avon. I knew it from the first— and I reckon you knew it too!'

She gasped, feeling hot colour flood her face. 'You must be mad! I acted as I would have acted for any man I did not wish to see unjustly convicted! It was only that and nothing, *nothing* more!'

'I won't take that.' His fingers tightened around her wrist. 'You're my woman, and I'll be coming to claim you when I've proved I'm innocent. Wait for me, Avon . . . and keep away from Carline.'

For a moment she was too astounded, too angry to speak, then her words came tumbling out.

'How dare you speak to me like that! I shall see Frank, or any friend, as often as I wish! You are completely mistaken in my—my feelings! You are nothing to me but a hunted man whom I have helped because I—I—'

'Because you like me,' he said softly, 'because you knew there was something special between us that wasn't meant to die. You won't escape me, Avon—and you don't want to!'

'You are impertinent! You mean nothing to me! I wish now I had never met you—and I intend to forget you and everything that has happened!'

'You do?' His voice roughened. 'Well, here's something to stop you forgetting me too quick!'

She was in his arms, held against his hard body, aware of the strong beat of his heart against hers. He kissed her, fierce, bruising kisses that shocked and frightened her—and sent a hot flame through her body. She ceased to struggle as her world rocked around her and she was caught in a primitive, searing emotion she had never known.

He released her abruptly. 'Someone's coming. Get back in the shadows.' He was astride the black horse in a second, leaving her to stare after him, too shaken to move or think.

The voices drew nearer and automatically she moved away as she tried to gain control over her agitation. Oh, how dare he! For him to assume she had acted as she did because she . . . liked him was insult enough, but to demand she wait for him, a man hunted by the law and hiding like a wild animal in the Indian Hills . . . Her hands flew to her hot cheeks. Would she ever be able to forget his kisses? In the train, she had been shocked and angry; when he had brought her back to the farm after the picnic she had been frightened of him and the passion she sensed in him. But now she had to fight the terrifying suspicion that something had leaped to life in her when his mouth touched hers, something that had answered his passion. He had declared she was his woman—and that she knew it! He was wrong! She had pitied him, as anyone would pity a hunted man about whose guilt there was still a question, that was all. It *must* be all. She would crush down this flame in her heart and forget Ken Grant—if she could!

CHAPTER
TEN

'I saw her come this way,' it was Daisy's voice. 'I guess she was feeling hot and took a stroll.'

'But that was some time ago,' Frank said. 'Could she have got lost do you think?'

Avon's hands flew to her hair, smoothing her disordered curls. Thankfully she grasped the explanation Frank had thrown out. As she moved forward, Daisy cried,

'Why, Avon, we've been looking all over for you! Frank was getting kind of anxious.'

'I got so warm I just had to cool off,' she said, relieved to hear herself speak naturally, 'and I'm afraid I was silly enough to lose my way in the dark.'

'You shouldn't have come alone,' Frank said, 'I would have been pleased to escort you any time. Supper is coming up.' He offered her his arm and she took it and they walked back to where the dancers were crowding around the laden tables.

'I must find the Mullers and Kate,' Avon said, looking around. 'I came with them.'

'I'll take you over,' Frank told her. 'I don't think they will mind if I join their party.'

'Why Frank,' Daisy paused and looked anxiously at him, 'Pheelie thought . . . I thought you were engaged to eat with us.'

Before he could answer, Avon took her hand from his arm, saying quickly,

'Oh, of course you must go, Frank. I can see the Mullers over there, waving to me.' She saw anger flash for a second in his dark eyes. 'Please,' she whispered, too low for Daisy to hear, 'they are old friends, you must join them if you are engaged to.'

He caught her hand. 'You'll dance with me after supper?'

'I shall be pleased to,' she assured him and hurried across the trampled grass to where the Mullers, Mrs Jonson and Kate and some of their friends—including Hank Garson—were sitting on buffalo rugs spread on a low bank. They greeted her gaily and she was grateful for the noisy chatter and laughter around her which gave her time to pull her thoughts together before anyone noticed her agitation.

The Skellar party was ensconced in the new carriage and there was a popping of champagne corks above the chatter. Pheelie's laughter rang out often and a little shrilly as she looked at Frank sitting beside her and Avon could not help wondering how long it would be before the pretty, enamoured girl would admit Frank was no longer victim of her charms. It would be a bitter realisation and her anger would be directed to the stranger she thought had supplanted her.

'But perhaps I have not supplanted her,' she thought. 'He has been attentive and I think he likes and admires me, but her possessiveness has annoyed him and he may wish to break with her and is using me to show her she no longer holds his affections.'

In her heart she knew this was not the true explanation. Frank, she suspected, was falling in love with her. Her thoughts were too scattered and her blood too stirred by her meeting with Ken for her to know if she were pleased or not. Ken had told her to keep away from Frank because he was jealous. A swift anger rose inside her; how dare he be jealous! She raised her head and saw Frank looking at her and smiled at him. If Frank loved her, it would be a gentle, sincere affection. With him she would always feel safe, cherished and respected, as a woman should be. He would never claim her love as a right or demand she recognise she was his woman.

He was at her side when the music struck up again and swept her into the barn and into a lively polka. She danced, talked and smiled, but they were mechanical actions. The charm of the dance was gone for her and she longed for the evening to end.

'It is stuffy in here, let us go outside,' he said. 'Can I get you some lemonade?'

She accepted gratefully, glad to leave the over-heated room where the dancers were getting rowdy as the last dance drew near. He brought her the drink as she stood in the shadow of the trees, letting the cool breeze refresh her.

'Avon,' she looked up, surprised at the urgency in his voice, 'When can I see you again? May I call?'

'We are busy just now,' she said quickly. 'Texas is away, and I have more to do in the house when my aunt helps Uncle Ben with the animals.'

'But I must see you,' he pleaded. 'Avon—you must know how I feel about you! You are so lovely, so enchanting . . .'

'Only because I come from England,' she said lightly, 'and I remind you of your home. Please do not say more.'

'But I shall, Avon, I must! I cannot help myself—'

'Frank,' Daisy had come up to them, 'Pheelie says for you to come over.'

Frank swung around and for a second his expression started Avon.

'Tell Pheelie I regret I cannot oblige. I'm sure there are plenty of young fellows only too eager to take my place.'

'But you'll be riding back with us?' Daisy asked, avoiding Avon's eyes. 'Pheelie said—'

'I am afraid your sister is mistaken, I am riding with the Mullers.'

Daisy turned away and Avon watched her go, feeling unhappy for her. Poor Daisy, who would have to bear the brunt of a sister's tantrums!

True to his word, Frank rode back beside the Muller wagon. Luckily, Mr Muller was feeling talkative and kept Frank discussing the recent harvest, the lack of success in catching the men rustling cattle and the prospect of the territory joining the Union, and Avon was left to fight off a deadly weariness that threatened to overcome her. She slipped from the wagon before Frank could dismount, thanked the Mullers and bade Kate and her mother goodnight, and hurried into the house, longing to be alone.

Rita had left a cup of milk warming on the stove and although she did not want it, Avon drank it, grateful for the thought. She did not expect to sleep, but the warm milk did its work and her tired body and mind relaxed as memory faded before deep and dreamless sleep.

She was having a late breakfast next morning and describing the dance for Rita when Sheriff Haskin rode up and accepted a cup of coffee.

'So you weren't down there last night, shaking a hoof with the rest,' Rita remarked.

He shook his head as he tossed his Stetson onto a peg and sat down at the table.

'I sure meant to, but something came up.' He looked across at Avon. 'Was it a good evening, Miss Avon?'

'Oh, yes, it was.'

'Must of been,' Rita commented. 'She slept till near ten and she's looking as lively as a wet chicken this morning.'

'She doesn't look that way to me,' Haskin said. 'I guess she wouldn't have had a dance to spare if I'd been there.'

'Of course I would,' Avon retorted. 'It would not do to get on the wrong side of the law.'

'Speaking of the law,' Rita said, 'when's it going to catch up with the gang stealing cattle? Henderson's herd has been thinned twice this month.'

'We'll get 'em.' He got up. 'Thanks for the coffee. I've a hard day ahead of me.'

'Chasing lawbreakers, I guess. You riding alone?'

'Yep. A posse is too easy seen.'

'Frank—Mr Carline—thinks the rustlers drive the cattle south and don't keep them in the hills,' Avon said, and saw the sheriff's face darken for a minute.

'Carline don't know everything,' he said briefly, 'he shoots his mouth off too much for my liking. I'll say good morning, ladies.'

When he had gone, Avon turned to her aunt. 'Why does the sheriff dislike Frank Carline?'

'For the same reason Carline don't blow kisses to Doug Haskin, and if you don't know the reason you're no wiser than a day-old turkey!'

Avon finished her breakfast in silence. Rita glanced at her as she hung up the dish-cloth.

'I reckon you're too wrapped in remembering compliments last night to fix the hog feed.'

'Of course not,' Avon jumped up. 'Texas showed me how.'

'Texas wastes more time chewing with you than he's worth.'

'But I miss him, Aunt Rita.'

Ben came back from Sweetwater with English letters for Avon. She read them, trying to keep her mind on their contents. She had kept busy all morning, refusing to let her thoughts take over, but she knew they were there, waiting to rush in with frightening memories.

The day dragged and she told herself it was her tiredness after the dance, but the same inertia was with her the next day, and the next. And she could no longer stop herself remembering. She felt her blood stir when she recalled the harsh, hungry kisses that had awakened her to strange and terrifying emotions, and she heard, again, Ken say: 'You're my woman . . . Wait for me, Avon.'

Because of what she had done, he took it for granted she must love him, that she would wait for him to claim her. He must be mad! Hiding deep in the lonely hills, avoiding all human contact, forever tense and watchful for pursuers, had twisted his mind until he saw in her actions reasons for thinking she loved him. He refused to believe she would have done the same for any man she wished to help escape possibly unjust punishment.

'To think anything so ridiculous—so completely impossible—to imagine I would ever think of him . . .' But she *was* thinking of him; she had been unable to banish his image and his words, no matter how hard she tried. 'It is because I—I dislike and distrust him,' she thought uneasily. 'His behaviour shocked and angered me so of course I cannot at once forget it. I hope I never see him again!'

Did she really hope it? A tiny doubt growing unheeded until now, swelled to frightening proportions as she stood staring out of her bedroom window into the darkening twilight. He had aroused anger, mortification and resentment in her and she hated him—or did she? Was it hate that had filled her with an excitement near to ecstasy when he kissed her so harshly? A feeling of panic caught her and she gripped her hands to her breast to still their sudden trembling as she faced the terrifying possibility she had been deceiving herself when she declared she felt nothing but enmity for this man, the sky rider, who claimed her.

She spurned the thought, only to have it return with greater force. Had she misjudged him? He was a man of hot blood, iron resolution, strong passions. He dealt in elementals. He had been branded a killer and he would follow a trail, no matter how lonely and dangerous to prove his innocence. What he wanted, he would fight to get . . . and he had said he wanted her!

No, she would not erect a false front of hatred and repugnance; she would not forget Ken Grant, something primitive had answered his passion and she would guard against its returning. She would fight memory no longer, to do so would only keep it alive. She would let her work, her growing attachment to her uncle and aunt and

interest in her friends fill her life—and there was Frank
Carline. The thought of his eloquent, dark eyes, his
eager words and barely restrained declaration was balm
to her heart as she turned away and she was conscious of
a desire to see him again and feel the protection of his
love.

Daisy came calling and Avon welcomed her. The girls
chatted about the dance; the dresses, hair styles and
behaviour of all the other girls were reviewed and
commented upon. Suddenly Daisy said,

'I reckon you won't know Pheelie's gone to visit in
Boston.'

'Why no, I didn't. I hope she will have a gay time there
and enjoy herself.'

'Ma thought she was looking peaky and made her take
Pain's Celery Compound, but Pa said she'd best be
away for a while where she'd get over Frank.' She
looked at Avon. 'Guess you know all about that, Avon.
I'm real sorry Pheelie feels as she does about you, she's
no cause to and mostly it's her fault. She's crazy about
Frank and won't admit he ain't riding herd on her any
longer.'

'Was he—fond of her once, Daisy?'

'Well, we all thought so. The cousins in Boston are
real social and Pheelie'll be too busy to think of Frank
Carline.'

'Oh, I'm so pleased you think that. I have been
unhappy about—'

'You've no need to, Avon. Pheelie had no chance
once Frank got his eyes on you. Do you like him?'

'Yes, very much. He is very popular, isn't he?'

Daisy straightened a fold in her riding skirt before
replying,

'I guess so, with most folk. Pa don't say much about
him but that's because of Pheelie, likely.'

'I have the idea Sheriff Haskin doesn't care for
him.'

Daisy laughed. 'Why you sly thing! Doug Haskin has

the same notions as Frank! Didn't you ever see two
steers locking horns?'

Avon jumped up. 'Come and see my flower garden.
Uncle has given me a little bit of ground and Texas
fenced it so the poultry can't scratch in it.'

Three weeks after the barn dance Texas turned up,
much to Avon's delight. He looked more weather-
beaten than ever and his horse had been ridden hard.
Ben welcomed him and Rita—to everyone's surprise—
baked a prune pie, Texas's favourite dessert.

'Sure is good to be back,' he said, and retired to the
bunkhouse after supper without saying more.

Avon pounced on him next morning after breakfast.
'Texas, where did you go? I want to know what you have
been doing.'

'Now Avon, Ben wants to set up a new wire fence
where the old one got broke up. I'll be working on the
boundary line all day and taking my chuck with me.'

'I'll bring you your food,' she said. 'I'll come a little
early so we can talk.'

When she came with his lunch, Texas straightened up,
tossing his wire-cutters aside.

'That looks mighty good,' he remarked, eyeing the
bread, sausage and remains of the prune pie. 'I'll eat first
and talk after, if you can hold your questions that long,
Ma'am.'

'I'll try,' she promised, and dropped down beside
him.

'Now,' she said, when he had licked up the last crumb
of pie and had reached into the pocket of his faded bib
overalls for the makings of a cigarette. 'I have an idea
you went south for a purpose, Texas. Am I right?'

He shook tobacco into the slip of paper. 'Well, there
was something kind of funny 'bout that ruckus in Tony's
saloon back in Laramie and I got the idea I'd mebbe take
a look-see and find if there was any folk as knowed more
'bout who was present when young Jones got hisself
rubbed out.' He licked the paper and sealed the cigarette

expertly. 'Seeing as you was so interested in the gent supposed to do the killing.'

Avon gasped as colour flooded her face. Was this another guess of his or did he knew more than she thought?

'I got thinking round that business at Olsson's farm,' he drawled, 'and it don't tally with me it were a gentleman pal as loosed him that night.'

Avon sighed and hugged her knees. 'So you guessed, Texas.'

'I reckon so, knowing you didn't cotton to the idea he did the killing. But you sure took a risk. What if Olsson, or the boys, had savvied something?'

'Well they didn't. They were going to take him to Sweetwater to be tried and hanged!'

'You was lucky—and by hokey, so was Grant. The law is sure hot to find him.'

'Texas, *did* you find out anything?'

He sucked in a mouthful of smoke and expelled it before answering.

'Yep, I found something. Jones was new to town. He was dead broke but he put out he'd a heap of money coming to him soon. He got drinking and the whiskey in him began talking and he boasted he'd information some gents would pay him good to keep quiet about. He got biggety with Grant who slapped him around a mite. Jones had handed his gun over the bar, him being a stranger and not knowing that kind of perlite behaviour ain't used much in Laramie.'

'How did the shooting begin?'

'There was some gents playing poker who got to arguing and broke up the furniture to settle it peaceful-like and sent a few playful shots through the roof and such and the barkeep swore he saw Jones heave a bottle at Grant and Grant drew and shot him.'

'He was lying!' Avon's eyes were blazing. 'I *know* he did not do it!'

'Looks like mebbe he didn't. The customers got out

quick when the fun started, but one man stayed and saw something.'

'Who was he? What did he see?' she demanded breathlessly.

'Name of Macky, an old trapper. I knowed him in Laramie and knowed he frequented that saloon and I visited his sister who told me Macky had hid behind the pianner that day and saw some shooting and lit out of town fast, him not being anxious to be present when the sheriff started asking questions.'

'But what did he see?'

'She don't know what. Macky rattled his hooves too fast for any conversation.'

'Then he may not know anything,' she said despairingly. 'And he has gone.'

'Well, no. Luck took a stake in the game, I reckon. Macky turned up while I was there.'

'You saw and talked to him? Oh Texas . . .'

'Aw, quit clawing my arm, Avon. Yep, I got him to admit he'd slid out of the saloon without being seen and he didn't know Jones had died and a man been accused of the killing.'

'*What did he see that night*?'

Texas dropped his cigarette butt and ground it into the dry earth with the heel of his boot before saying slowly.

'He was mighty tight-lipped about it with me, but he says he saw who killed Jones—but he wasn't spilling no names. Macky had a run-in with the law away back and he ain't anxious to remind the Laramie lawmen he's around. But he gave me the strong notion it weren't Grant as done it.'

'Texas, that man—Macky—*must* tell what he saw! He can prove Ken is innocent! We must get and *make* him speak!' She sprang to her feet, her cheeks scarlet with excitement. 'You must go back to Laramie!'

'Quit fussing. Macky had business in town but he said he's riding this way and he's willing to speak out to the sheriff here. Likely he'll mosey along any day now. Thanks for bringing the chuck. You tell Rita she can bake another prune pie any time she's a mind to.'

CHAPTER
ELEVEN

THE time had come for fall house-cleaning and Avon was kept busy scrubbing out cupboards and washing shelves and blankets. In the evenings she helped her aunt to cut up worn-out garments into strips ready for the winter rug-hooking. There were berries to be made into jelly, corn to be dried and ground, vegetables to be pickled and beef dried to make 'jerky', a staple food during the winter. At night she was too weary to think or plan how the information Texas had given her could best be used. He had been definite in forbidding her to say anything to Haskin.

'Once old Macky is here we can loosen up,' he told her. 'Keep a close mouth, Avon, no good'll come of talking too early. Grant's pretty safe in the hills, I reckon Haskin don't know 'em as well as he does.'

'Ken said there was something going on in those hills and he meant to find out what it was.'

Texas shifted his wad of tobacco. 'Mebbe he's right, at that.'

Avon did not try to analyse her feelings, they were too complex, too disturbing to her peace of mind, and too dangerous to dwell on. She was no longer sure what she felt about Ken Grant. The excitement she felt at hearing what Texas had discovered did not tally with a desire never to see him again. But she most surely did not love him. He had come into her life so strangely, had disrupted it and forced her to be aware of him and wish to see justice done, but he would fade from her life once he was freed by the law. If indeed he should come to 'claim' her, she would send him away in no uncertain manner, she told herself.

But it was difficult not to long for someone to confide in. Texas had refused to discuss the matter and was busy on the farm all day, and it would be most unwise to say anything to her uncle or aunt who might ask uncomfortable questions. Yet it would bring relief from the endless uncertainties and unanswered questions that beset her if she could only disclose something of them to a trusted friend, someone who would see things from an impartial angle, who was free from prejudice and would advise her.

She was thinking this as she washed out the milk pans one morning and heard steps and a voice call: 'Anyone at home?'

She turned to see Frank smiling at her from the kitchen door and suddenly she had her answer.

'Frank, I am glad you have come.' She dried her hands quickly and came to him.

'Is something the matter, Avon?' His dark eyes searched her face. 'You look worried, a little strained. Have you time to talk with me?'

'Yes, my aunt is in Sweetwater with Texas.'

He pulled out a chair for her and seated himself on another beside her.

'I hate to see you bothered about something, Avon. Can't I help? Won't you tell me? You know I am ready to do anything I can.'

She did know it, his eyes told her, and his voice. Impulsively she said,

'Frank, the man wanted for a killing, Ken Grant . . . People say he is hiding in the Indian Hills, that he is the sky rider. Sheriff Haskin is looking for him.'

Frank's brows had drawn together in a quick frown.

'Haskin is very busy in the hills these days, he is warning people to keep out of them. Yes, I've heard of Grant but I do not suppose it is true, he would be out of the territory by now. Murder is a hanging-matter and he would not risk staying anywhere for long.'

'But if he is not a murderer?'

'What do you mean? He killed an unarmed man down in Laramie last year, there was a witness, the barman swore to the killing.'

'But there was another witness who did not swear to it.'

'What do you mean?' Frank asked sharply.

'There was an old man called Macky who hid when the shooting began and who saw what really happened. He did not wait and he has been missing all this time and didn't know Jones had died and Ken been accused.'

'Who told you this?'

'I can't tell you that, Frank, but we both feel sure Macky knows who really did the killing. Frank, I am certain now that Grant was the victim of a plot.'

She waited with beating heart. She had taken him into her confidence and already a faint apprehension as to the wisdom of it was making her uneasy. But his next words put her fears at rest.

'If all this is true,' Frank said slowly, 'then Grant was surely framed. But why should someone want to kill a young cowboy passing through town and doing nothing worse than getting rowdy drunk?'

'Possibly because of what he said when he was drunk. He spoke of knowing something that was to bring him a lot of money, it sounded as if he expected to be paid for keeping silent about something.'

'In fact, blackmail,' Frank said contemptuously. 'I suppose it could be something like that, although it is not really very likely.'

'I think the barman was bribed to bear false witness against Grant who had already had some trouble with Jones,' she told him. 'The truth will be known when this man, Macky, comes. He said he *saw* who did the killing.'

'And he is coming up here soon?' Frank asked. 'Is that what you mean?'

She nodded. Already she felt a burden had been shared and she had been right to confide in Frank. 'Quite soon.'

Frank's fingers tapped the table as he regarded her thoughtfully.

'Why didn't this man tell what he saw as soon as he knew Grant had been accused?'

'He disappeared without waiting to find out what had happened. He has only recently returned from his wanderings.'

'Why does he come up here? He could give information in Laramie, if he really has any of importance.'

'I suppose he has his reasons. But once he is here Sheriff Haskin will—'

'—will do nothing!' She started at the sudden harshness in his voice. 'Haskin has been riding the Indian Hills for quite a while, saying he's trailing Grant, but he hasn't brought him in, has he? And he hasn't managed to put his finger on the rustlers that are stealing our cattle. He rides alone—and I think I know why.'

'What do you mean?' she asked sharply.

'Avon, Haskin isn't to be trusted. He served a prison sentence in Mexico which is something people here don't know. He's sheriff of Miles City, yet he is hanging around here most of his time, *why*? He is in a position to know what is happening and where herds are being moved to, isn't he?'

'Frank!' She sprang to her feet and faced him. 'Surely you don't think he has anything to do with the rustling of cattle?'

Frank too had risen, his eyes cold and hard as steel.

'There is a very clever man at the back of crimes in this part. The law has not caught up with him, maybe because the law does not wish to.'

'I cannot believe it! I am sure he wants the rustlers caught and intends to get Ken Grant too. But once he knows Ken is not guilty—'

'Why are you interested in this man Grant?' Frank's eyes searched hers intently. 'You have never seen him.'

'Yes, I have.' Quickly she told him of the meeting in

the train. 'Of course, I did not know who he was then.'

'You have never said anything of this before.'

'I realised he wanted to get away before the sheriff came. I did not say anything because—because I was so startled and frightened by the train being attacked. And I did not wish to be the means of a man being caught by the law.

'And you let a murderer escape!'

She raised her chin, meeting his accusing gaze firmly. 'I do not believe he is guilty, and I think this man Macky's evidence will prove it, Frank.'

He was about to speak when there was the sound of the buggy returning. Rita's eyebrows rose when she saw Frank follow Avon out onto the verandah, but all she said was,

'Help me with these packages, Avon—and treat that one mighty delicate seeing it's the pair of shoes you've made me buy 'gainst my better judgment. Howdy, Carline. Holiday time at the Two-Bar again?'

'Just calling in on my way to the city,' he said easily.

'Taking the long way round, ain't you? Take a look at the back wheel, Texas, seems it don't run too easy.'

Avon had plenty to occupy her mind for the rest of the day. She was shocked and disturbed by Frank's suspicions of the sheriff being involved in rustling. And yet it *was* a little odd that so little had been discovered. Did Haskin know where the stolen herds were hidden and was he haunting the Indian Hills, using his search for Grant as a pretext to stay in the district? Was he the brain behind a gang of criminals? She found it hard to believe. Yet Frank had been so sure. There was enmity between the two men, she knew, but Haskin was a man sworn to uphold the law and to search out lawbreakers and bring them to judgment and it was horrible to think he might use his powers for his own, criminal ends.

She decided to say nothing of this to Texas. He had told her not to speak of Macky and she had disobeyed him. She knew she could trust Frank, but Texas might not think so. He had never shown any particular liking for the 'greenhorn from England'.

She had no opportunity to talk to Texas until next morning when the laundry line broke and she called him to repair it.

'When is old Macky coming?' she whispered.

'Could be here any day.'

'Texas, exactly *why* didn't he want to give his evidence in Laramie?'

Texas squinted at her irritably. 'Sure like to know every nail in a boot, don't you? Females is squirrel-curious. Macky wanted me around when he says his bit; there's a few wrinkles in his past he's a mite uneasy over.'

'I wish he would come. Texas,' she glanced around to be sure they were out of earshot, 'I think Ken Grant should know about Macky coming.'

'Oh sure,' Texas spat disgustedly. 'We'll send up an Indian smoke signal calling him down from his skyline to take tea with us social-like!'

'Indians!' She straightened up, her eyes going to the jagged hills breaking the skyline so sharply in the clear fall sunlight. 'That squaw, Wana, knows Grant, she once brought me a present from him. I think she could get a message to him. How can I reach her?'

Texas was silent for a few minutes while he made the clothesline taut. At last he said,

'Wana has a son, they call him Seeing Eye. I saw him in town today.'

'Can I reach him? Oh dear, I'm afraid I will miss him if I wait until Uncle Ben goes into town next.'

Texas wound up the unused bit of clothesline carefully, keeping his eyes on it as he said.

'Likely there's a chance he'll drift down this way tonight.'

'To the farm? To see you?' she demanded eagerly. 'But why?'

Texas's leathery face assumed the bland, innocent expression she knew meant anything but innocence.

'Well, it's this way. Seeing your aunt don't see eye to eye with me on the subject of a man's having a thirst water don't do no good to, Wana's boy kindly offered to tote a parcel from town.'

'You mean, you asked him to bring you some whiskey,' she accused him, beginning to laugh, 'and he will come tonight when no one will see.'

He grinned at her. 'I reckon Rita's got eyes that can see through paper or sacking so I dasn't take no chances with her. I'll give him a message if you're so set on it, but you're riding dangerous ground, Avon. Grant ain't free of the law yet.'

'But he soon will be. I'll write a message and Seeing Eye must see Ken gets it as soon as possible.'

She no longer asked herself why she was so eager to have Ken Grant's name cleared. She could not lie to herself and pretend her burning interest in the fate of this man, the lonely sky rider whose image refused to be banished from both her waking and her dreaming hours, was simply a wish to see justice done. She had not forgotten him as she had hoped to do. She heard his voice and saw him, standing tall and stern, as he said: 'You're my woman . . .' She had tried to hate him and failed; she had tried to forget him and was aware of him to a degree that frightened her. She was not in love with him, she *could* not be! It was impossible she could feel love for a man of whom she knew so little. She had become obsessed with his romantic history, and by the fact she had twice come to his help. He was a fever in her blood which would work out once he was a free man and had ridden away to wherever he had come from. She knew nothing of him, where his home was, where he had worked before the killing in the saloon. He had ridden into her life and, for a time, dominated it, and she must wait for prudence and common sense to restore her to a clear realisation of her folly. Ken, she told herself, would go out of her life, but the bleak dismay the thought brought her was no comfort.

Kate rode out to spend a day with her, glowing with happiness and pride.

'I guess you'll know why, Avon. Hank's spoken for me and Ma says we can marry in the spring.'

'Oh Kate, I am so happy for you both! This is wonderful news.' She pressed her friend's hand. 'I am afraid your mother will miss you.'

'Ma's going to give up the rooming business, she's saved quite a bit and she's going to help Mrs Muller in the store, it's what she'll like doing. Hank will have the ranch someday, Bill's all set to join his uncle running cattle up from Texas.'

They spent a cheerful day discussing Kate's future. As she was leaving, Kate said,

'Now, when are you going to get yourself fixed up with a husband, Avon Meredith? There's Frank Carline and Doug Haskin butting horns over you. Have you made your choice yet?' Avon shook her head, smiling. 'You got half the boys around here dreaming over you. Ain't you decided to pick one of them?'

'I have made my choice,' she said solemnly, 'I shall marry Texas!'

Kate shrieked. 'My, you sure are close-mouthed! But I don't blame you. Tell me when the wedding bells are set to ring for you—and good luckl.'

So far, there had been no sign from Grant in return for Avon's note. Seeing Eye, a slim, taciturn Sioux youth, had agreed to deliver it and Avon waited in vain for a reply. It was now over a week since Texas had said old Macky was on his way and her impatience was growing with every day.

Rita had noticed her restlessness and let her off some of her chores so she could take the pony out for a gallop in the brisk fall air that was beginning to hold a tang of the approaching winter. Her ride always took her in the same direction, where she could see, from a rise in the

land, the road snaking between hills southwards. And
still Macky did not come.

She had finished drying the dishes after supper and
was sitting on the verandah when Sheriff Haskin rode
out of the dark. He dismounted and after tying his
mount to the hitching post, came up the steps.

'Evening, Miss Avon. I was passing and thought I'd
look in.'

'I'll call Uncle Ben, and I'll make coffee,' she ran her
eye over his dusty clothes. 'You look as if you have had a
hard day, sheriff.'

'Something like that,' he agreed, pulling off his hat
and mopping his forehead. 'Coffee sure sounds good.
I've been down in Bittercreek Valley, there's been a
shooting there.'

'Oh? Who was it got shot?'

'Some stranger, an old fellow called Macky. Someone
shot him as he crossed the creek. Seems he knew Texas,
that's why I've called in.'

Avon felt the blood leave her face as a chill crept over
her.

'Is he . . . is he badly hurt, Sheriff?'

'I'm afraid he's dead, Miss Avon.'

CHAPTER
TWELVE

FOR a moment Avon's brain refused to take it in. She stared at the sheriff with eyes dilated in horror and dismay. It could not be true! All proof of Ken Grant's innocence lay in what the old trapper had seen and was willing to divulge—and now his secret had died with him!

. Through stiff lips she asked: 'Why was he killed? Who could have done it?'

Haskin shrugged. 'I've no answer for that. It isn't likely an old fellow like him would have enemies, but there might be something in his past. Maybe he was mistaken for another man, that is the likeliest, I'd say.' He turned as Ben came out of the house. 'Is Texas around? I want to see him.'

When Texas came up the steps the sheriff told him briefly how he had heard shooting and found the old man dying from a head wound.

'He must have been shot shortly before I came up, I'd been camping nearby. He had a few papers on him, one with your name on it.'

Texas listened without a muscle moving in his brown, leathery face.

'Sure I knowed him once in Laramie,' he said. 'We wasn't buddies, Macky kept a close mouth about hisself. He changed trapping for prospecting out West.'

'Did he have any enemies?'

Texas shook his head. 'Never knowed of any.'

'You'll ride with me to Sweetwater to identify the body.' Haskin turned to Avon. 'Reckon I'll give that coffee a miss. We'll be getting on to town.'

She watched them go, her heart a leaden weight in her breast. Now Macky was dead, she knew how much she had been counting on his revealing the truth.

'You're looking upset,' Ben said. 'Sit down and rest. This is a bad business. It seems a senseless killing. We'll hope Haskin will get to the bottom of it.'

When she went to her bedroom that night she sat for a long time staring unseeingly out at the moonlit night, caught in a tumult of feeling that allowed no subterfuge, no specious argument to hide the truth. To prove Ken Grant innocent of murder, to see him free and no longer an outcast, had become the most important thing in her life. The shock of Macky's death, the only witness who could save Ken, swept away all her defences and in a blinding flash of self-knowledge she knew she had tried to convince herself she hated Ken because she was afraid of him! Afraid of his virile, dominant masculinity that had called forth such a frightening response in her when he had held her in his arms! She had determined to forget him, but it was impossible. He was far off, riding the bare ridges of the Indian Hills at night, watching and waiting, yet he was forever with her, in her mind, her memories and—was it possible—in her heart!

Texas was back the next day but he avoided Avon, evidently not wishing to discuss Macky's murder. Avon's thoughts were continually on Ken: what would he think, buoyed up by what she had written to him, when he knew all his hopes were dashed? Her heart ached for his disappointment and she felt she must see him and the longing grew as two days passed without news. When at last the sheriff came it was to tell them the old man had been buried and the killing remained a mystery.

Rita noticed Avon's shadowed eyes and the restlessness she could not hide and when they were alone, she said,

'You've something on your mind, Avon. I reckon you

don't mean to tell me and you don't have to. But if it's worrying you some, and if Ben and I can help, remember we'll do our best for you, always.'

Avon turned away, feeling tears prick behind her eyes. There was a gentleness in Rita's voice that touched her deeply.

'I'm sorry, Aunt Rita, but it is something I cannot tell you, not yet. I *have* been . . . upset and I—I wish I *could* tell you . . .' She bit her lip. How could she tell her aunt and uncle she feared she had given her heart to a man hunted as a killer? They would be shocked and see only the danger of her interest in such a man. She must keep her secret.

Texas's behaviour dismayed her. He refused to speak of Macky's death and did not seem to have any further interest in Ken and the killing in Laramie. Avon, after one or two attempts to talk to him, gave up in bitter disappointment. It was obvious he would be no help to her if she wished to get in touch with Ken. He was no longer her friend and confidant and her heart was sore at his cool indifference. She began to wonder if she could find Wana and so get a message to Ken, but no one had seen the Squaw.

She was in Sweetwater, having driven in with her uncle, when she caught sight of a slim, brown figure entering the dry goods store. She hurried after him and found him standing fingering some bright cotton materials.

'Come with me, Seeing Eye, I want to speak to you.' He stared at her without replying. She pointed to the cloth: 'You want to buy some of that?'

'My mother like. Is too much money,' he said.

'If you will do what I want I will give you money to buy some.'

His eyes, black and opaque, met hers and he nodded. 'I come.'

He followed her out of the store and down a narrow side lane.

'Seeing Eye, I want you to give a message to the man you call the sky rider. You know him?' The boy nodded. 'As you did once before. And bring me his answer. You are sure you can find him?'

'I find.'

'How?'

'I find,' he repeated.

'Tell him I must see him, it is important. He must tell me where and when I can meet him. You understand?' She saw Ben driving the buggy down the street and hastily pressed some money into the boy's hand. 'Bring me his answer. You know who I am?'

'I savvy. I come at night, at window.' He turned and ran back into the store.

Now she was caught in the toils of a burning impatience, wondering if the message would reach him, and if she had been rash in asking to meet him. Was he still in the hills? But Seeing Eye seemed certain of finding him.

Three days dragged by and her impatience mounted to fever point. Perhaps the Indian boy had taken her money and forgotten her message. Or Ken had decided to seek safer territory. Her heart sank as she reviewed the possibilities. If she never saw him again . . . But she must! He had said he would claim her; but he would never claim her while men hunted him and there was a price on his head.

Then one night, as she lay sleepless, staring into the dark, she heard a faint tapping on her window. For a moment she thought it was a loose shutter, but there was no wind. She jumped up and ran to the window. The night was black and she saw nothing, but a voice whispered,

'Man send this.' Something was thrust into her hand. There was the faintest movement in the dark, then all was still.

She drew the curtain and lit the candle with fingers that trembled. The tiny pellet of paper opened and she saw the words: 'Picnic valley. Across creek. Sunday. Wait for me.'

She slept little that night. Somehow she must get permission to ride out to the hills, but how? Ben and Rita would never let her ride alone for a whole day—and they would ask questions.

'I *must* see him,' she thought as she turned restlessly in her bed. 'I must find some way.' A sudden thought came. 'Texas! I will ask him, beg him to come with me.'

She followed him down to the creek next morning when he watered his horse before riding off to work at the far end of the farm lands.

'Texas, you have got to help me . . .' The words came tumbling out in her eagerness to persuade him. She told him of Ken's message and of her determination to meet him in the picnic valley. 'I cannot go alone, my uncle would not allow it, I fear. But if you came, all would be well, Texas.'

He jerked the horse's head up from the water and turned, his eyes—those keen, dark eyes that missed so little—searching her face ruthlessly. She knew he had seen the swift colour in her cheeks, but she met his gaze without flinching.

'Just how much does he mean to you, Avon?'

'A great deal, Texas. Enough to determine he shall not die for a murder he did not do! I have told you everything because I trust you.'

'Well I ain't ever let you down yet, have I?' He climbed stiffly into the saddle. 'Tell your aunt and uncle I've promised to take you to see the Sioux camp come Sunday. I'll notify Ben you've wore me out pestering me to see it.'

'What a clever idea! I do thank you. Texas, you haven't spoken of it, but you must have been as shocked as I was when poor Macky was shot. Have you any idea who could have done such a thing?'

'Well it sure weren't a friend,' he said briefly, and rode across the creek, leaving her in the bright sunlight with the wind teasing her curls and the skirt of her pink gingham gown billowing around her slender form. Her eyes were gentle as she watched him go. Texas was still her friend and he would help her. It was the death of Macky that had upset him and made him so uncommunicative. She could trust him to keep her secret.

Ben looked dubious when Avon spoke of the ride to the hills.

'Texas said something about it, but it's a long ride and you'll be out all day and—'

'Let her go,' Rita directed a sharp look at her husband. 'Avon's been looking peaky and a day in the open would pick her up. Texas can take care of her.'

'I would be so interested to see an Indian camp,' Avon said quickly. 'I would like to see how the squaws do their beadwork.'

'I'll pack food for you both, riding's hungry work— though you ain't been much interested in food of late.'

Avon thanked her gratefully; she had not expected things to be made so easy for her.

That evening, when they were sitting on the verandah after supper, Rita said abruptly,

'I don't aim to be nosey, but I've one question: are you fixing to meet Frank Carline?'

Avon sat up. 'Meet Frank? Of course not, Aunt Rita. Anyway he is gone away again, Kate tells me.'

'He'll be back, though I'd like to know what takes him off work so much. Ranchers ain't known for having itchy feet, work keeps 'em pretty close to the ground.'

'Frank has his man, Red Jessup, to manage the ranch when he is away.'

'Me, I wouldn't let Jessup manage a graveyard 'less he'd rob the graves,' Rita snapped. 'Frank sure is a trusting soul to hire a man like that. Come to that, none of his hands are plumb popular in Sweetwater. Haskin's had to slap down on 'em more than once.'

Avon hesitated, then made up her mind. 'Aunt Rita, do you know Doug Haskin well?'

'I guess so, he kept law in Sweetwater before he went to Miles City.'

'Where did he come from before that?'

'Mercy, child, how'd I know that?' She shot a glance at Avon. 'You interested in the gent?'

'Oh no, I just wondered. Frank does not like him.'

Rita sniffed. 'Me, I'd choose Doug before pretty-boy Frank.'

Avon laughed. 'Well I'm not choosing anyone, at least not yet.'

Friday crawled by. Saturday seemed to have double the number of hours, hours for Avon to dwell on her meeting with Ken, on what he would say, how he would look, what were his plans. But Sunday came at last, with a vivid blue sky and sharp sunshine and a quick breeze.

The night before, Ben had said: 'You'd best take my horse, Blazer, your pony's not game for so long a ride,' and now Blazer was pawing the ground, restless to be off in a gallop. Texas packed the saddle bags with the food Rita had given them and swung himself into the saddle.

'You see she don't get into any trouble,' Rita called from the front steps.

Texas snorted. 'Women and trouble is like fleas and scratching, you got one, you got t'other.'

As they rode off Avon remarked on the fine weather and was surprised when Texas shook his head.

'Too good too early,' he said, 'that wind'll bring up rain cloud.'

She refused to believe him. Excitement filled her heart and with it came a joyous expectation. She was to see Ken again! It made the world beautiful in a way she did not seek to explain. The sunlight and blue skies were an augury that all would be well. Some further information—another witness, remorse on the part of the barman—would turn up and Ken would be a free man, free to claim her as his woman! Her heart sang as she rode.

She recognised the trail they took as being the one Ken had ridden when he brought her home from the valley on the night of the picnic. She was lost in memories of that night when Texas asked abruptly,

'What d'you plan to tell Grant?'

'Everything that has happened. He must be told old Macky has been killed. Texas,' she rode closer to him, 'how is it the Indians can find Ken when no one else can?'

'Grant caught a man roughing up Seeing Eye and scared him off and Wana was right grateful to him, though being a Sioux she don't say nothing. It's my guess she and her folks have helped Grant, fetching him food and such.'

'If I see her I shall thank her. I wonder why anyone wanted to hurt her son.'

'He didn't get his name for nothing. Ain't much goes on in those hills he don't see. He's got eyes like a young eagle, and he's mighty clever with bow and arrow, no one can touch him in killing game for the tribe, I've heard.'

The hills seemed to come to meet them as they rode, their ragged outline naked in the sunlight and melting into the dark line of trees on the lower slopes. The odd, twisted formations fascinated Avon; deep canyons, narrow shadowy ravines, abrupt escarpments and shelving plateaux, and the turbulent streams that had carved their path through the rock in ages past.

Texas told her the Indians, Cheyenne and Sioux, had retreated into the hills before the advance of the white men and the range held few secrets for their descendants who had returned to the plains when wars had ceased and the invaders triumphed. A few Indians had chosen to remain in their hill camps and these were mostly Sioux.

It was near midday when they rode into the valley she remembered so well and crossed the stream to find a place to eat their meal. Texas watered the horses while Avon unpacked the food. Ken said she must wait. Perhaps he was already watching from some ridge above. Her eyes searched the heights but found nothing.

After they had eaten, Texas said: 'Reckon I'll keep out of sight awhiles, Grant mightn't show hisself if he sees a stranger.'

'I have thought of that. Of course I will tell him you are a friend and we can trust you. I expect he will want to ask you about Macky.'

Texas washed the dishes in the creek, then packed the bags and retreated through a thicket of willows, having at first picketed his horse out of sight. Avon settled down to wait, trying to calm her quivering nerves and control the uneven beating of her heart. How long must she wait? How would he greet her? Would he rebuke her for putting him at risk?

Pictures filled her mind: meeting his vivid blue eyes on the train; the sudden grim anger in his face as he hit the robber; his kiss before he slipped away; firelight picking out the strong planes of his face after he had found her in the valley; the feel of his hard body as she rode behind him; when she had met him at the barn dance . . .

The sun passed its zenith and began its slow downward journey. Texas was invisible. Blazer drowsed, head hanging, in the shade, his only movement the impatient flick of his tail to ward off flies.

Avon rose and strolled up the creek, too restless to sit still. Sunlight was thinning as wispy trails of cloud began to fill the sky. She walked to the stepping stones where Frank had caught her to prevent her falling. The lupins were over and the creek ran deeper after the recent rains. The wind sharpened and she tied her scarf more tightly around her head.

When would he come? Her eyes began to ache as they searched the hills. She could not afford to stay too late, Ben and Rita would be worried even though Texas was with her, and she had promised to be home before dark. She looked uneasily at the thickening cloud above her, remembering Texas's prophesy of rain.

A sound made her swing around. A horseman was riding down the valley, his hat pulled low over his eyes.

Her heart leaped and she started to run forward. Suddenly her steps faltered. Something was wrong; the horse was a sorrel!

Too startled to move, she watched the rider draw close and rein in his horse.

'Wal, if it ain't the pretty little lady in the train that interfered with a bit o' business I aimed to finish!' The jeering words were like a whiplash. Horror gripped her as she saw him sweep off his grim Stetson with mock respect, revealing a brutish face disfigured by a long birthmark on one cheek!

She stared up at him, fear chilling her body and numbing her brain. What was he doing in these hills? No one had seen him since he had slipped away from the Two-Bar ranch. Frank was of the opinion he would make for Mexico.

She had no idea where Texas was. Probably he was not far off and would come if she called. Her eyes went to the rifle in its scabbard in the saddle boot and the gun thonged down on his thigh, gun-fighter style. Texas was unarmed.

'It sure ain't right a pretty girl should be alone in this place.' He grinned as he slid from the saddle. 'I was allus fond of ladies' company. Me and you can have a little pow-wow over old times.' His face changed abruptly as he came towards her. 'You little hell-cat! Saw me on the train, did you? And had to spout your mouth out to Carline!'

'Yes,' she stared at him defiantly although she trembled, 'and you ran away. If you had not, you would be in jail now!'

'And you'd be feeling real bad about it, wouldn't you?' he jeered. 'You tell me something, who was the punk who smashed my jaw?'

'He was a stranger to me.'

'If him and me ever meet up agin he'll get what's coming to him! You done me out of a good line of work, lady, and I reckon you'll pay for it now!'

'Texas!' she called as she whirled about to race back the way she had come, grateful for the divided skirt and stout boots that did not impede her wild flight. She heard the man swear and heard his heavy tread behind her, gaining on her! Her foot caught on a stone and she stumbled and fell—and heard the sharp whine of a bullet as she lay trying to get her breath back! She raised herself and looked back to see the man crouching down, staring upwards. She followed his eyes and her heart jolted inside her breast. Where the walls of the valley ended in a pine-clad plateau, a great black horse stood as if carved from ebony! Its rider moved slightly and she saw the glint of light along the barrel of a rifle trained on the crouching man! Another shot sent echoes up the valley and the man sprang to his feet and raced for his horse which plunged nervously. A third shot kicked up a spurt of dust behind him as he flung himself into the saddle and dug spurs into the horse's sides. The terrified animal crossed the creek in a bound and crashed through brushwood and out of sight just as Texas came running.

'What in hookey . . . You hurt, Avon?' he was kneeling beside her.

'No, I am all right. That man who has ridden away was the train robber, he escaped from Frank's ranch and must have been hiding in these hills.'

Texas helped her to her feet. 'Seems Indian Hills is getting plumb popular,' he said dryly and turned his head to squint up at the horseman who had not moved. 'That your friend?'

'Yes,' she said breathlessly. 'He must have seen the man chasing me and shot at him to scare him away.'

'Sure is a pity he warn't a better shot,' Texas said grimly. 'Such vermin don't deserve to live. You sure you're all right? You'd best sit down and take a nip of whiskey.'

'Oh Texas!' She laughed, feeling herself relax as fear left her. 'Did you bring some?'

'Ain't never without it,' he told her. 'Best medicine

for snake bites and fainting females anyone knows. You take a sip—and don't let on to Rita.'

The raw spirit made her splutter and cough but it warmed her and she was grateful for it. Ken had gone and for a moment she wondered if he would not come now he had seen Texas. Would he suspect her of trying to trap him? Oh, surely not! Her breath came quick and hard as she listened. Texas listened too, his head cocked.

He came riding up the valley, Darkie stepping delicately. Avon, watching him, felt her heart thud against her ribs and her breath catch in her throat. He was coming to her, the man she had tried to hate! Her whole being seemed to reach out to him and her heart cry: 'Yes! I am your woman!'

He reined up beside them, his eyes, stern and wary, going to Texas.

Avon said swiftly: 'He is my friend, I could not have come without him. He knows everything and we can trust him.'

The men locked eyes for a brief moment, then Ken nodded and slid from the saddle.

'Glad to know you. Avon, were you hurt by your fall?' The vivid blue eyes she remembered so well rested on her anxiously.

'No. Did you recognise the man? He was the train robber who tried to shoot you.'

Ken nodded. 'I knew him.'

Texas spoke for the first time. 'Reckon you didn't aim to get him.'

'No, he might be—useful.'

Texas's eyes narrowed for a second as he stared at Ken, then he turned, saying over his shoulder,

'I'll water Blazer, he's acting kind of restless.'

They watched him go, then Ken turned to Avon. The bones in his face stood out under the taut skin and there was a two-day stubble on his chin. His shirt was sweat-stained and torn and there was blood on one sleeve.

'Nothing to count,' he said quickly as Avon's eyes widened in dismay, 'Someone got to practising shooting and I was in the way.'

'They were trying to shoot *you*?'

He stared down at her, a muscle in his jaw twitching slightly.

'Would it matter to you if they were?' his voice was harsh. 'Isn't it right that a murderer should be shot and save the law the job of arranging a hanging?'

'But you are not a murderer!' she cried. 'There was a man coming who knew who did the killing, only . . . Oh Ken, he has been killed!'

He caught her arm. 'Sit down and tell me, Avon.'

She told him, and saw his face tighten. When she had done, he sat silent beside her, his eyes on the ground and his face telling her nothing. At last he raised his head and looked at her. 'Who else knew Macky was on his way here?'

'No one but Texas and . . .' she broke off, remembering. 'I did tell Frank Carline, he is a friend and I trust him, Ken. He has always been kind and helpful. Could he have told someone? About Macky, I mean. But why should anyone want to kill the old man? He would have been able to clear you and save the law from making a terrible mistake. Everyone must want that.' Her voice died to a whisper as she saw his face.

'Everyone except the gent who did the killing,' his eyes were ice-cold and bitter, 'and his pals. It sure was a frame-up. There must have been more men in it and none of them would welcome Macky's evidence.'

'You think they are here?' she stammered, 'that they waited for him? Frank *must* have talked! Oh—how *could* he! Ken, I wanted to tell Sheriff Haskin, but Frank does not trust him for some reason. He thinks he may be behind these robberies. Haskin does seem to be behaving oddly—and Frank says he once served a prison sentence in Mexico.'

'That doesn't necessarily make him a criminal, many

men have a shady spot in their past but learn better ways.'

'Then you don't agree with Frank?' ·

He rested his elbows on his knees and stared down at his clasped hands.

'There is cattle thieving going on and I'm pretty sure now the herds are hidden in these hills. The gang have a hide-out, they must have. I've seen something—and I think the Indians know something only they're afraid to speak. Two Indians have disappeared in the last two weeks and I caught a man beating up young Seeing Eye who says he saw some riders who disappeared.'

'Disappeared?'

'The boy could find no trace of them later. Avon,' his hand closed over hers in a hard, warm clasp, 'keep out of this. This is dangerous work. Don't come here again.'

'But Ken, I want to help you, *you* are in danger.'

His lips twisted in a wry smile. 'I reckon I'm about used to it now. I can look after myself. I've an idea I'm on to something important and I'm not quitting yet.' His eyes searched hers. 'Why did you come today, Avon?'

'To tell you about Macky and—and—' she met his intent gaze, '—and I wanted to see you again!'

He bent forward, his face tense. 'Does that mean you care what happens to me?'

'You once said I was—I was your woman,' she said it softly and felt hot blood race through her body as she saw the leap in his eyes.

'You refused to believe it! You were all set to forget me—quick!'

'I found I couldn't. I—I thought I hated you, but I know now I never did.'

He slid his hand under her chin, turning her face up to his. She trembled as she met the blaze in his eyes.

'Avon, does that mean . . .'

'It means I'll be waiting for you, Ken,' she whispered, and putting out her hand she touched his lean, tanned face with gentle fingers.

He caught her hand. 'Avon, sweetheart! You mean that? If I get out of this mess . . . My uncle in Dakota offered me a job as ranch foreman, I was on my way there when trouble broke in Laramie. He'll hold it for me. He's set to make me partner one day. We'll have a home and—' His head jerked up as a light footfall caught his ear. Avon turned swiftly and saw Seeing Eye beside them!

'I find place,' he said, his eyes on Ken. 'You come now.'

Ken rose swiftly, pulling Avon after him. 'I've been waiting for a break like this. I guessed there was a hiding place in these hills and I reckon he's found it! You must go back.'

'No, I will not!' Her chin high, she looked at him with resolute eyes. 'I am coming with you. If there is danger—'

'No much danger,' Seeing Eye said. 'I find safe place for see.'

Ken caught her hand in his. 'You mustn't be mixed up in this.' He raised his head as Texas rode up. 'Take her back, Texas. The boy has found something and I must go with him.'

'Best do as he says, Avon,' Texas advised, 'this ain't no work for women.'

'I'm going with Ken, the boy says it is safe. You can go back if you wish, Texas.'

Texas shrugged. 'Reckon it ain't no use arguing with a female woman. We'd best move pronto, them clouds look angry.'

'Avon, I insist . . . Hell, Texas!' Ken turned an exasperated face to Texas who was unhitching Blazer, 'make her see sense.'

Texas muttered something about 'women don't *have* no sense,' and helped Avon mount Blazer. Ken hesitated, then shrugged and unhitched his own horse and the little cavalcade moved off with the Indian boy riding ahead on his shaggy pony. Avon's heart was beating fast.

She was sharing Ken's danger, taking a part in his life. Nothing would prevent her following him, he was her man and at last she knew it!

CHAPTER
THIRTEEN

ONCE out of the valley the going became rough. The horses scrambled and slithered up a steep slope, sending loose stones rattling down behind them. At the top, the ground levelled out for a time, then came a descent into a ravine thick with low scrub and stunted willow. Another ridge, then down into a narrow gully.

Avon's nerves tightened painfully and she left it to Blazer to find his way down the rocky ledges and loose red earth to the bottom. There they forded a creek before following the Indian boy to an abrupt cut in the cliffs that led them into a wider valley whose rocky walls were fissured and gashed by harsh winters and blazing summers. She had lost all sense of direction. The sun was now hidden behind sullen cloud and a sharp wind whined down the valley, scattering the yellowing leaves of the cottonwoods bordering a straggling creek bed. They seemed to have been crossing ridges and following canyons and threading groves of red fir for hours and still Seeing Eye rode ahead, his eyes never still as they searched the peaks above them.

'Sure is hell's own country,' Texas growled as his horse missed a footing and stumbled. 'No cattle could of come this away.'

'No,' Grant agreed, 'but it's the right place for a gang to hide out from the law.'

'And you reckon the boy's found it?'

Grant nodded and turned to Avon. 'Are you tired, honey?'

She assured him quickly she was not. He glanced ahead and said sharply,

'He's signalling us to wait.'

Seeing Eye rode up. 'I go see, you stay,' he said and turning his pinto he rode swiftly through the trees and out of sight.

Texas said abruptly. 'I reckon it's time you come clean about what set you on this trail, Grant.'

Ken eased himself in his saddle, pushing back his wide hat as he said,

'I guess so. I broke jail in Laramie with the help of a pal who staked me to a horse and money and I picked up the trail of the men who'd framed me. The barkeep swore they had cleared off before I shot Jones, but I knew that wasn't so. They hadn't worried to hide their tracks, thinking me safe in the hoosegow. Someone laid me out in the saloon . . . and the bullet that killed Jones came from my gun. That sure told against me.'

Texas grunted, not without admiration. 'That sure was quick thinking, using your gun for the killing. Weren't no other witnesses around?'

Ken shook his head. 'I guess not, they all got out pronto when trouble began—except the real killer and his pals. The barkeep swore blind he'd seen me fire at Jones—and there were men who'd seen me slap Jones down earlier when he got frisky with me.' He rested both hands on the pommel of his saddle, staring down at the grass Darkie was cropping. 'My horse was stolen after I'd missed the trail and gone too far east and I took the railroad to hit Miles City because I'd a hunch the gents looting banks and holding up trains could be connected with Jones's murder.'

Texas nodded. 'I reckon Jones was going to split on 'em and ha to be rubbed out.'

'And the only man who saw the real killer and was ready to speak out is dead!' Avon burst out. 'Texas, you *must* tell the law that Macky knew something!'

'Aw, Avon, who'd believe me? Macky didn't say anything to pin on nobody. He said he'd spill it to Sheriff Haskin here.' His leathery face hardened. 'And me, I don't reckon to tangle with the law 'less I have to.'

Ken shot him a swift glance. 'I guess Texas is right. And the way the law looks at it, my breaking jail proved me to be the killer.' He looked up. 'The boy is waving us on.'

They left the belt of pines and made their way down a shelving trail and into a steeply walled canyon through which ran a wide shallow river that washed against the fissured rock towering above, shutting out much of the light and producing a curiously ominous atmosphere. The harsh walls seemed ready to close in on unwelcome strangers and Avon shivered, aware of something sinister and dangerous about the place. A cold wind was snaking down the canyon, bringing a misting rain, and she was grateful for the slicker Ken had made her wear. She rode close behind him, her eyes on his broad shoulders. If there was danger she would share it with him; together they would fight for his freedom and to see justice done.

Texas had stopped to stare around him. 'By hookey! You could run a herd through this water and leave nary a trace! Where does it come out, Grant?'

'Close by the south pass. I don't know where the water rises, or how they get the cattle in, but it's my guess they drive 'em through here and cache 'em somewhere near the pass and move out at night.'

Seeing Eye beckoned them on impatiently. They rode through the water, the men's eyes alert for signs of cattle or horsemen having passed this way. From Texas's grunts he found confirmation of his suspicions and a chill of excitement, mingled with fear, crept over Avon.

Suddenly the Indian boy swung his pinto to the left. They had come to a narrow gorge, a split in the canyon wall, half filled with driftwood carried down by winter overflow. Beyond lay a small thicket of scrubby trees and beyond that again, a wall of rock enclosing the gorge.

With some difficulty they reached the trees where they dismounted and staked out the horses before going back to a place among some bushes from where they could watch the river, yet remain unseen.

'You stay,' Seeing Eye commanded them. 'Can see.'

'See what?' Texas demanded, but the boy did not answer. He had moved forward and was peering out from the cover the bushes gave him. The canyon wall across the river was furrowed and split as if by some giant's knife, holding dim clefts and sudden spurs of rock. Trailing vines hung from many crevices and swung in the wind. With the grey light and thin whistle of wind the place had a nightmarish hostility that struck fear into Avon's heart and made her draw close to Ken. His arm went around her, holding her close against him.

'The boy's waiting for something—or someone,' he muttered. 'We're hidden from sight and the wind will cover any noise we make. You're trembling, sweetheart, are you scared?'

'Yes, terribly,' she admitted. 'There is something horrible about this place, Ken. What do you expect to discover?'

He looked down at her, his lean face grim. 'I know there's a hide-out somewhere in these hills—'

'No speak!' the Indian boy whispered. He was straining forward, his eyes raking the rocky wall opposite. Suddenly a sound rose above the wind's whine, the ring of metal on stone. Avon felt Ken's body stiffen and heard Texas's smothered exclamation.

Out from the very cliff wall, it seemed, a horseman rode and paused at the water for his horse to drink while he glanced casually right and left before rolling himself a cigarette. Then he jerked the horse's head, crushed his hat more firmly on his head and rode slowly down the stream until a spur of rock hid him from view.

Avon gasped and her fingers bit into Ken's arm as she turned to stare up at him.

'It was Red Jessup! Did you see? Is he one of the criminals too, like the man with the birthmark? They have been using Frank's ranch as a blind! We must warn

Frank; he's in danger!'

'How come he rode smack out of the rock face?' Texas demanded.

'Small cut in rock,' Seeing Eye said briefly. 'Come see.'

Ken released Avon. 'Stay here while I take a look, honey.'

'Oh, don't go, Ken, please don't go! It is too dangerous!' She clung to him. 'There may be others!'

He stooped and kissed her swiftly. 'I'll go carefully, I promise.'

He followed the boy, splashing across the river. Avon watched him, her hands clasped and her breath coming fast as fear gripped her. If anything should happen to him . . . if Red Jessup should return . . . or another member of the gang . . .

'By hookey, they've gone!' Texas exclaimed leaning forward. 'Must be a break in the rock hid by them creepers and bushes, a break just wide enough for a man and horse—and cows—to pass through!'

'But where does it go to?'

'If Grant's right, to a mighty neat little hole-up for rustlers and mebbe other gents wanted by the law.' Texas's eyes were alight with excitement. 'Riding through water don't leave no trail. When they've drove stolen stock south at night they can return and set nice and cosy till things settle down.'

'They are coming back,' Avon breathed thankfully.

'We'd best get moving,' Ken said tersely as he came up. 'The boy smelt fire smoke up the gorge. It's a narrow cut in the cliff and it's my guess it opens into a valley where there's a camp.'

They retreated swiftly to where they had left the horses. Ken helped Avon mount, then swung himself up on Darkie and led by the boy they set off. No one spoke until they were out of the canyon. Something in the place, a brooding threat, hung over it, pricking nerves to jumping point. Avon knew both men were uneasy by the way their eyes searched the trail and the quicker pace to which they urged the horses.

The rain, now heavy, did not make the terrain easier to ride. When Blazer's foot slipped, Avon clenched her teeth to prevent a cry of fear. Ken rode near and she knew he watched her, but he did not speak until they had reached even ground when he pulled up and said,

'Seeing Eye will take you the rest of the way, I've got work to do.'

'Ken,' Avon rode close, her eyes seeking his, 'you won't take any chances? These men are killers, they are evil! I am afraid for you. You will be very, very careful, won't you?'

A sudden smile warmed the bleakness of his face. 'Sure I'll be careful, Avon sweetheart, now I've everything to live for!'

'Reckon Carline's been a mite careless in taking on hands,' Texas said, rasping a finger across his bristly chin. 'Him being away so frequent sure made it easy for Jessup and his pals to play safe at the Two-Bar.'

'We must warn Frank—' Avon broke off, startled by what she saw in Ken's face.

'No!' It was a command. 'Any hint, any movement on his part, will alert the men. Neither of you must say a word of what we saw today. Understand?'

'Reckon you're right,' Texas agreed. 'Are you going to notify the sheriff?'

Avon's heart skipped a beat as she remembered Frank's suspicions that Haskin was connected with the criminal activities in the area. *Could* he be the man whose brain planned crimes, using his position as a cover? She longed to ask Ken but there was not time. Already he had gathered up the reins.

'Look after her, Texas.'

'Wait, you must take your slicker,' she pulled off the yellow oilskin and gave it to him. 'It has stopped raining. Ken, when will I see you again?'

'I can't say for sure.' His face was sombre as he looked

at her. 'I'll let you know just as soon as I can.'

'Like Avon says,' Texas said, 'don't go taking no chances. You're up against something big, I'm thinking. Keep your gun tied low, son.'

Ken nodded, raised a hand in farewell and swung the black horse into a gallop. Avon and Texas watched him go.

'Texas, I'm frightened.' Avon shivered. 'He is up against ruthless men.'

'Yep, but now he knows where they hide, and they won't savvy he's watching. Grant's learned Indian ways, I reckon.'

'But what can he do . . . What can *we* do? If the sheriff discovers something, he will arrest Ken. Texas, do you trust Haskin? There are—people who do not.'

'Meaning Carline? Shucks, Avon, Haskin and Carline are both sweet on you and ain't to be trusted. A man in love is plumb loco. Carline's got his bristles up and wouldn't see no good in Haskin if he growed wings and a halo.' He kicked his horse. 'Time we moved, your folk'll be riled at getting in so late.'

It was with a heart and mind full of frightening thoughts that she rode with him and the Indian boy down into the picnic valley and out at last into the foothills. She had left Ken to face danger alone when she longed to share it with him. But there was nothing she could do, no way in which to help. She must just love him, pray and wait.

On the ride back all her thoughts were of Ken, the man she had come so surprisingly to love, the man who was now her whole life. *Was* there any way in which she could help him? If she went to Frank . . . But Ken had forbidden her to speak of what she knew. She could not bring her uncle into what might be a dangerous show-down between criminals and the law. Texas? She remembered his reluctance to 'tangle with the law' and wondered if there was something in his past, some incident he did not wish resurrected. Texas was no gunman but it was possible he had had a brush with the law in his younger days.

Rita was on the verandah as they rode up and as Avon slipped down from Blazer, aware of aching muscles and deep weariness, she said,

'Child, you're all tuckered out!'

'I'm only a little tired, Aunt Rita. I am sorry we got delayed, but Texas looked after me well.'

'He's kept you out a lot too late. You'll have eaten nothing since noon; I've kept your boiled bacon and greens hot.'

Avon's longing for solitude and sleep was almost overwhelming, but she fought it back and managed to eat some of the supper her aunt had kept for her. Ben came in and asked,

'Well, Avon, did you spend all your money on Sioux beadwork?'

For a second she was bewildered, then she caught Texas's eye and remembered the reason she had given for her ride to the hills and hastily explained she had not cared enough for any of the work to buy it. Soon afterwards she pleaded weariness and retreated to her room.

At first her mind was too full of images for her to sleep. The disfigured face of the train robber, the lone rider on his black horse with sunlight striking his rifle, Grant's gaunt, tense face and the light that blazed in his eyes when he saw her, the perilous trek through the hills to the shadowy canyon and the astonishing appearance of Red Jessup. Questions teased her tired brain. Would Grant try to penetrate the hide-out and what would he find if he did? To whom could he give information on what he had found if he was still a hunted man with a price on his head?

When sleep came it brought frightening dreams that made her start up in her bed, trembling and chilled with dread.

She awoke early next morning, but Ben and Texas had

already breakfasted and gone into the fields by the time she came into the kitchen where Rita was washing Ben's overalls.

'Eat your food,' she said, picking up the washing basket, 'I'll be back to talk to you.'

Avon's eyes followed her uneasily as she left the kitchen. Had Rita guessed her visit to the hills had nothing to do with seeing the Indian village? What did she want to talk about?

She did not have long to wait. Rita returned, poured herself out a cup of coffee and sat down at the table and looked at Avon for a long minute during which time Avon's uneasiness increased.

'Doug Haskin was here yesterday, Avon, and he didn't look happy to know where you'd gone. I asked him outright what was keeping him in Sweetwater and he said he was hunting a killer in the Indian Hills.'

'I knew that, Aunt Rita.'

'Well I asked a heap of questions and he said this man Grant was on the train you come by and was in your coach and skipped before help came and you hadn't no recollection of how he looked or exactly when he slipped his halter.'

Avon met her eyes without flinching. 'What of it, Aunt Rita?'

'I ain't no fool, Avon. You take note of people—but maybe you were shook up by the hold-up.'

'Yes, I was.'

Rita planted her elbows on the table and looked at Avon across the rim of her cup.

'Well it's my guess you weren't too shook up to notice a good-looking young fellow sitting opposite you, it purely ain't natural. You've a soft heart, maybe too soft for this country. You clammed up when Haskin asked questions 'cause you didn't want to help a man get caught by the law. Ain't I right, Avon?'

Avon drew a deep breath and reached for the coffee pot.

'You are right. I did not know why he was unwilling to meet the sheriff, but I did guess he wanted to escape and I was not going to give him away—to anyone.'

She ended on a note of defiance and saw a grim smile touch her aunt's lips.

'Like I said, you're too soft for this land. I ain't busting with brains, but I've known something was on your mind and you're worried and unhappy. Me and Ben don't aim to let you get hurt if we can help it; you've come mighty near filling the hole Minna left in us. Is it something to do with this man, Grant, that Haskin's after?'

Avon put down the cup she had just filled and raised her head to meet her aunt's dark eyes, her mind made up.

'Yes, Aunt Rita. Ken Grant is not a murderer. He was framed by men who had reason to kill someone they thought could betray them to the law. I am certain a witness was bribed to accuse Ken.'

'Wasn't there no one else saw what happened?'

'Yes. A man saw the killing and was on his way to tell what he saw—and he was shot before he got here.'

'That old fellow, Macky?' Rita put down her cup abruptly, staring at Avon. 'That sure smells bad, him being bushwhacked that way. You reckon someone's set to see Grant hanged for what he ain't done?'

Avon nodded, aware of a deep relief in confiding in Rita. She had been wrong in thinking her aunt would condemn her. She leaned forward impetuously.

'I know Ken is innocent. He followed the men who did the killing and I believe he has found them. He is determined to prove his innocence, and I will help him all I can!'

'I guess you've been meeting him,' her aunt said slowly. 'You've played a mighty dangerous game. You never said nothing to us—'

'I was afraid you would be angry, and would not believe Ken is innocent. I'm sorry, Aunt Rita, I should have known better.'

'Maybe it's my fault,' Rita rose from the table. 'I'm no good at letting on what I'm feeling and I was cruel hard on you when you first come. You got a liking for this fellow Grant?'

'Yes!' Avon sprang up and went to Rita and caught her by her arms. 'I love him! I didn't know it at first, but it is true. I shall do everything in my power to help him get free. He is my man!'

Rita's black eyes searched her face fiercely. Suddenly they softened and she said,

'It comes that way with some women. I knew Ben was for me before he did. You've taken on a heap of trouble, child, and I'm worried sore for you, but me and Ben'll help any way we can, you can count on that.' She bent and kissed Avon awkwardly on her cheek. 'Reckon Haskin will get at the truth soon, he don't say much but he ain't easily fooled. Now you can clear the table and after, wash the dishes and iron them two shirts of Ben's. Murder and crime and love don't stop chores being done!'

CHAPTER
FOURTEEN

THE days following her ride into the hills were deeply anxious ones for Avon. Her fear for Ken's safety increased daily when she got no news from him, and she was tortured with visions of his being discovered while keeping watch on the robbers' hiding place. Red Jessup and the man called Dexter were both ruthless men, neither would shrink from shooting the man they may have tried to get hanged for a murder committed by their gang. She grew pale and thin and her grey eyes, so often turned to scan the great range of hills, had dark shadows beneath them.

Rita said nothing when Avon set aside most of her food declaring she had no appetite and watched, without comment, the restless activity that gave her no peace.

What was happening in those hills outlined against the clear, cold autumn sky? What secrets did their coulees and treacherous escarpments hold? If Ken found proof of cattle being hidden, would he call in the law and risk being arrested? Her fears never left her and her heart was hungry for Ken. When would she see him again?

She returned from a walk along the creek bank one morning to find the Skellar surrey hitched to the rail in the yard and Texas squinting at it contemptuously.

He jerked a horny thumb at the house. 'You got elegant company visiting. Reckon they had to get dicked up in their Sunday clothes 'fore they could sit in that fancy contraption.'

'Is it Mrs Skellar?' she asked.

'Sure is, and Pheelie and Daisy along with her. Rita's mad as a trodden cat 'cause she's been caught washing floors in her sack apron.'

'Well, I'm not dressed for company either,' Avon sighed, 'but I don't intend to take off *my* apron.'

'That there pinny looks a heap better'n Pheelie's get-up. The poor girl's cinched up so tight she can't breathe natural.'

Avon could not help smiling at his disgruntled expression.

'It's that elegant carriage of theirs; you're jealous, Texas! You'd love to drive it.'

'Me sit up in that tiddly little trap?' Texas spat scornfully. 'I'd sooner ride an Arizona mule!'

She left him, still smiling. She had not seen Pheelie since she had returned from Boston where she had become engaged to a wealthy young lawyer and was wearing, Kate told her, a diamond ring as big as a marble. She hoped Pheelie had got over her spitefulness now she had lost interest in Frank Carline.

Mrs Skellar and Daisy greeted her warmly and Pheelie smiled graciously and toyed with the ruffles at her neck to show off her ring. Rita, sitting stiffly with her hands folded on the unfortunate sack apron, turned a bitter eye on Avon and told her to make coffee. When she returned, Pheelie was describing the social life of Boston while her mother regarded her with fond approval.

'I'm sure I'm pleased you enjoyed your visit east,' Rita said, 'though it ain't my idea of pleasure.'

Avon drew Daisy aside. 'What good news about Pheelie's engagement, I am so glad she has found happiness.'

Daisy did not speak for a minute, then she said slowly, 'I'd like to think she is happy, Avon, but . . . Well, I'm not all that sure.'

'Not happy when she is going to be married?'

'I wouldn't say this to a soul but you, Avon, but I think she's still sweet on Frank Carline.'

'Oh, you must be wrong. She has forgotten him, I am sure.'

Daisy shook her head doubtfully but said no more.

As the smart little equipage drove off with its new paint gleaming and the silken fringe fluttering, Rita stared after it and snorted furiously.

'Dressed up fancy for a morning visit—and me swilling the kitchen floor!'

'In that horrid old apron.' Avon untied it dextrously. 'I'm putting it in the stove, Aunt Rita. You have plenty of nicer aprons. If you had only asked me I would have washed the floor.'

'You work hard enough,' Rita touched her cheek. 'You're thinner. You're worrying about that man of yours holed up in the hills, ain't you?'

'Yes, I do worry dreadfully,' Avon confessed as tears filled her eyes. 'What can I do, Aunt Rita? How can I help? I love him so much!'

Almost shyly, Rita's arms went around her. 'I reckon there's nothing any of us can do but wait. My guess is Doug Haskin is up to something. He's been away quite a while, maybe he'll have news when he gets back. Doug won't want to hang an innocent man, Avon, even if it spoils his chance with you to prove Grant never did the killing.'

'He never had a chance,' Avon murmured, 'I have never loved anyone but Ken.'

'Well, that settles Frank Carline's hopes too—and I ain't sorry. Set the table for supper, I hear Ben in the yard.'

Avon suspected Texas was avoiding her and it saddened her that she could no longer discuss her hopes and fears with the tough little man she had come to like and trust. Probably he thought her fears well founded and her hopes likely to be dashed. In this rough life, justice was not always done and criminals, when caught, were swiftly tried and punished to discourage others who might think of taking to a life of lawbreaking.

When Frank rode up one afternoon she was pleased to see him. He was someone young and cheerful to talk to and help her keep her dark fears at bay.

'You look tired,' he told her as he took a seat beside her on the steps where she sat washing eggs in a bowl of water. 'Does your aunt make you work hard?'

'Of course not,' she assured him. 'Maybe I'm not yet accustomed to this climate. Are you very busy on your ranch now?'

He answered absently, his eyes on her face which had a wistful expression new to him. Avon was thinking how she would have liked to confide in him and ask his advice—and warn him against Red Jessup. But Ken had forbidden her; and there *was* that uncomfortable suspicion that Frank must have spoken of old Macky's arrival to someone. If Jessup had known, he might have suspected the old man from Laramie of having a purpose in coming to Sweetwater and decided to kill him. The thought haunted her and she shivered.

'Avon, is anything troubling you?' Frank asked abruptly, and taking the bowl from her he set it aside and caught both her hands in his. 'I cannot bear to see you looking sad. You have to work too hard here, it isn't the life for you, you are not used to this rough life, you need someone to look after you, to care for you!'

Warned by what she saw in his face she said quickly: 'Oh, I am happy here, truly I am. My aunt and uncle are good to me and I am learning to love this country. But—' she hesitated, '—but there *are* bad men, rustlers, robbers and criminals here, aren't there? It frightens me sometimes.'

'You are perfectly safe, Avon, your uncle has no cattle to be stolen.'

She could not help asking: 'Do *you* think there are gangs hiding in the hills?'

'No, only the odd lawbreaker making for the south. Have you been worrying about it, Avon?'

'I suppose I have.' She withdrew her hands gently. 'I have been in those hills and men, cattle, *could* be concealed there.'

'Who has been telling you such tales?' His face was

suddenly stern. 'Avon, I don't like your going riding in those hills. As I have told you, it *is* possible a few badmen might be roosting there for a time. Promise me not to go again.'

'I don't go alone, Texas comes with me.'

'That old fool! He couldn't use a pea-shooter!'

'Sheriff Haskin rides in the hills—'

'—looking for a lawbreaker, he says.'

'Frank, suppose the man, Ken Grant, is not guilty? He could have been framed.'

'You're crazy, Avon. Why should you think that? You saw him only for a short time in the train.'

'He—he did not look like a killer,' she bit her lip, wishing she had not spoken. Frank was regarding her intently.

'You are too soft-hearted, Avon. You've built up a romantic picture of an innocent man being hunted down. Grant is a killer and you may be sure he has killed before. God knows why that fool Haskin hasn't caught him before this—unless it would interfere with plans of his own! Oh Avon!' He caught her by her shoulders, making her look at him. 'You are wasted here! You are too lovely, too sweet, too desirable! My dearest, you must know how I feel about you. From the first time I saw you I—'

'No, Frank, please do not say it.' She sprang to her feet in dismay. 'I—I do like you, but I do not and cannot ever love you. Oh Frank, I'm sorry if I have hurt you!'

He rose too and stood looking hungrily at her flushed face, dark curls and the soft curves of her figure.

'I am not hurt,' he said. 'I have spoken too soon, too abruptly and I have startled you. I love you and want you more than any woman I know and I mean to have you. I shall wait, Avon.'

'No, no! It will be useless, please believe me!'

'I do not believe you, my sweet. My love is too strong for you to escape me. I shall *make* you love me!'

She heard her aunt's voice in the passage and turned

swiftly and ran down the steps and around the house to the stable yard where Texas was coiling fencing wire. His bushy eyebrows rose as he saw her agitated expression.

'Please saddle my pony, Texas, I'm going for a gallop.' Without waiting she hurried into the house to change into her riding skirt. The desire to get away from the house, from Frank and his protestations of a love she did not want, was overwhelming. Texas helped her mount and watched her ride off across the fields with puzzled eyes.

She let the pony have its head, feeling her nerves relax in the exhilaration of the gallop. The cool wind that swept her seemed to blow away some of her distress at having to reject Frank, although her distress would have been greater if he had not been so arrogantly sure she must in time return his love.

When at last she returned, Rita said abruptly: 'Frank's gone. He high-tailed out of here like he'd a burr under his saddle. I can make a guess why—but I don't aim to ask questions.'

'I fear I had to—to disappoint him, Aunt Rita.'

'It won't do him no harm to get a set-down,' her aunt said unsympathetically. 'Seeing you're dressed for riding you can take this note over to Mame Skellar, she won't give me no peace till I let her have my recipe for salt-rising bread, hers ain't fit to feed hogs.'

Avon took the note, guessing her aunt was deliberately giving her a respite from housework, and set off on her pony for the Skellar ranch where Mrs Skellar made her stay for a meal.

'The girls will be back anytime now,' she said, 'and they'd be sad to miss you. Pheelie's giving out invitations for her engagement party and she's one for you.'

'Thank you, Mrs Skellar. Will Pheelie's fiancé be able to attend it?'

'He's all set to be with us 'less something important holds him in Boston, but Pheelie says she'll hold the party anyways. Her aunt in Boston has sent her a real elegant gown.'

Avon was not sorry when the girls failed to appear. She would have liked to see Daisy, but had no wish to meet Pheelie. She was wondering how she could avoid the engagement party when Mrs Skellar remarked,

'You'll be sure to come, Avon? Daisy'll be purely disappointed if she don't see you here, she thinks a heap of you.'

Before she left, Avon had promised to attend the festivity, although reluctantly. She was in no mood for parties, her heart was too heavy, her thoughts too anxious for her to enjoy society.

There was a full moon that night and after helping with the dishes, Avon slipped a shawl around her shoulders and walked down to the creek. The light was like a ghostly twilight and the shadows were black and thick. Her eyes went to the Indian Hills so stark and menacing in the cold light. She had a vision of Ken on his great black horse poised against the purple vault of sky, the mysterious sky rider, watching and waiting, seeking proof that would free him from the law. When could she go to him? When could their love be open and free? When could their lives be safe and their future secure?

A faint sound made her turn sharply to see Seeing Eye behind her. He held out a slip of paper.

'Sky rider send. You send message by me.'

Trembling with excitement she snatched the paper from him.

'I will write the answer as soon as I have read this. Come to my window.'

He nodded and followed her, his feet making no sound, silent as a shadow.

'My dearest love,' Ken wrote, 'I must meet you again but I can't come to the farm yet. Meet me on the west side of Old Butte tomorrow as near to sunup as you can. You have my heart always.'

She read it with fear and joy. He was risking much to leave the hills and ride as far as Old Butte, a strangely-shaped, flat-topped hill rising over six hundred feet from a tangle of rock and trees. But to see him again, to read the love in his eyes and his tanned face, to feel his hungry arms around her and meet his kisses with a passion matching her own . . . She must tell him she would meet him. Quickly she wrote, folded the note and went to the window where the Indian boy waited, his sleek head turning alertly at every sound. He slipped her note inside his leather pouch and set off without a word and was lost in the shadows.

She sat down to plan. She would have to rise shortly before the sun was up. If she saddled her pony now it would save time. She would leave a note for her aunt, and take some food for Ken. She waited until Rita and Ben had gone to bed, then stole into the kitchen and filled a bag with bread, cheese, beans and some bacon. She decided it was too risky to saddle the pony, Texas might hear her, and went back to her room to sleep fitfully for a few hours.

Everything went smoothly. No one heard her steal from the house and her pony was quiet as she led him from the stable, keeping well away from the bunkhouse where Texas slept. Once over the creek, she set the pony to a sharp gallop, trusting him to follow the trail in the faint light. All her thoughts were with Ken, her whole being was alight with anticipation of their meeting. He was her man and she loved him and no matter what the future held, she would always love and follow him.

The sky slowly lightened as she rode. Low cloud on the horizon flushed to a rosy pink and then to gold as the night shadows fled before the glory of the rising sun. The air was sharp and sweet and she felt at one with the gradual awakening of the world to another day, and hope filled her heart until she could have sung with joy! All was going to be well! Ken would be freed of his wrongful accusation and the true killer found. Mysteries would be explained and difficulties swept from their path!

Old Butte came in sight, rising abruptly from a jumble of rock, trees and scrub, a craggy cone left when erosion had done its work. Avon let the pony pick its way through the bush and around to the western side where she dismounted and tethered it to a tree before leaving the wood. It was unlikely anyone would be abroad at this hour, but it was wiser to keep the pony out of sight. She climbed a low hillock and sat down, her eyes on the trail that ended in the great range of hills, beautiful in their garments of dawn.

He came from a side trail, riding Darkie swiftly across the grassy plain. She saw him turn his head and told herself fiercely that the day would soon come when he need not keep alert for enemies or the law.

She went to meet him. He flung himself from Darkie who snorted and shook his head before turning to nibble the grass.

'Ken!' She threw herself into his arms and felt them close around her as if he never meant to let her go. She could feel his heart beating strongly against hers and for a long minute the world and the bright dawn faded around her as she lay against his breast.

'Avon, my own little sweetheart! My God, at times I've been plain crazy to see you!' He bent his head and kissed her, hard hungry kisses of a man starved and longing for her love.

Time stood still for them as the sky flamed and then melted into palest green that merged into a sapphire dome arching above them. The pony snickered and Darkie raised his head in answer. Avon sighed and let her hand rest on Ken's brown cheek as she murmured,

'I thought I was never going to hear from you, Ken. I've been so frightened, wondering where you were and what you had discovered.'

'I couldn't let you know before,' a muscle tightened in his jaw. 'I was busy—and I had to be careful. I've found out plenty, Avon. The stolen cattle are cached in that hidden ravine, it's a cinch for hiding men and cattle, the ravine widens out and it's well watered.'

'Ken, you didn't go into it?' she exclaimed.

'I sure had to, Sweetheart, if I was to know the set-up there. I reckon I ran it a mite too close once—but Darkie can outrun any cayuse in the county.'

'Someone saw you? Oh Ken, you should not have risked it! Did you see who it was?'

'Yes, it was the gent who took such a fancy to your little watch in the train and who would have rubbed me out if you hadn't knocked his gun up.'

'Ken, you *must* be careful! He remembers you and said he wants to settle with you. It must be his gang that is doing all these crimes.'

Ken shook his head. 'He's sure a badman, but there's someone with a better brain than his back of all this. It's my guess the men who framed me are holed up in that ravine and Jones was once one of them. Maybe they turned him off and when he got the notion of blackmailing them—and collecting the head-money—men were sent down to Laramie to smoke him out. Avon,' his arms tightened around her, 'you don't know how good it is to see you! When I didn't get a message I figured you couldn't make it, but I came on the chance.'

A chill crept over her as she pulled away to look up at him.

'But—I sent you a note by the Indian boy to say I would be here, didn't you get it?'

He frowned as he stared at her. 'Why no, I never saw the boy after I'd sent him to you. You say you sent a note back with him?'

'Yes, I did. Ken, what could have stopped him? He has never failed before. Did he forget, or not trouble to find you?'

'No. His people have been good to me, they've given me information, though they're scared of the gang.' He was silent for a few minutes, his mouth set in a grim line.

'You must get back, you'll be missed. Your folks will wonder—'

'No, I have told my aunt about you. I know I can trust her and my uncle.'

'That's good news. But you'd best get back. I'll ride you part of the way.'

'It isn't safe for you—' she began, but he had left her to fetch up her pony.

They rode in single file out of the trees and through rough, hilly ground at the base of Old Butte. To the south, low rocky hills broke the grasslands and Avon turned her pony saying,

'It is less open that way and safer, though it will take longer.'

It would give her a little more time with Ken before the pain of parting.

He kicked Darkie into a trot, his keen gaze sweeping left and right as they left the trail. Some of his tenseness communicated itself to Avon and she, too, found herself watching and listening uneasily.

They had left the grasslands and were making their way between two sparsely wooded hills when Ken's horse snorted and pranced to one side nervously. Ken cursed and jerked the rein. Avon felt her pony hesitate and, looking to one side, she called out,

'Stop, Ken! There is something in those bushes!'

He swung out of the saddle before she had finished speaking and was crouched, gun in hand, beside her while his eyes raked the scrub in which something moved.

'Get down and stay behind your pony,' he snapped out the order. As he began to move forwards, she cried,

'Be careful!'

She watched from the shelter of the pony and saw him stoop suddenly and heard his startled exclamation.

'Ken, what is it?'

'It's Seeing Eye—and he's hurt!'

She ran to him as he kneeled, running his hands over

the boy's brown body. Seeing Eye looked up at him, his dark eyes blank with pain.

'Ken, he's been beaten!' Horror rose in her as she saw the cruel weals across the brown chest and the cut, stiff with dried blood, on one cheek. 'Who could have done it? Is he badly hurt?'

'No bones broken,' he said grimly. 'I reckon he's weak from loss of blood. Who did it, boy?'

'Bad white man . . . Bad face . . .' his hand stole to one cheek, then dropped. Light broke on Avon and she said quickly,

'Was it a man with a red mark on one cheek?'

The boy's eyes glazed with pain and weakness, met hers and for a second she saw something fierce and untamed blaze in them. Then they dropped and Ken said,

'I'll wash the blood off him. Have you anything—'

'Take my blouse,' she pulled off her jacket and removed the cotton blouse and gave it to him. 'Ken, he must be hungry. I have the food I brought for you, I'll get it.'

'I'll get him to eat something, and tie up those cuts, and take him to his camp, his folks have medicines. You must get home, Avon, before Texas comes hunting you.'

'I don't want to leave you!'

He looked up. 'Sweetheart, you must. I'll find a way to meet again but you've got to get out of here.'

She realised he suspected the boy's attacker might be lurking, or might return, and fear filled her heart. But she knew she could be of no use to him, he would attend to the boy's hurt and return him to his people.

He went with her to her pony and before he put her into the saddle, kissed her hard and fiercely. Then he slapped the pony's flank and it sprang forward.

She rode back beset with fears and questions that had no answers. Did Ken suspect, as she did, that the Indian boy had been deliberately waylaid and the message he carried stolen? She had seen the empty pouch flung aside on the ground. Had someone guessed his errand? Perhaps she and Ken had been seen meeting! Her veins turned to ice as she pictured Ken being followed and attacked as he took the injured boy back to his camp. She shut her eyes, sick with horror—and heard a horse's thudding hooves ahead of her!

With startled eyes she watched her uncle ride up on Blazer. He did not speak until he had turned to ride beside her, then he said,

'Your aunt has told me everything, Avon, and I read your note. I don't like the look of any of this, you're running into bad trouble, maybe danger, meeting this man Grant who's wanted by the law. I'd have prevented you, had I known. You're in my care now.'

'I know I am, Uncle Ben, and you and Aunt Rita have been wonderful to me and I shall ever be grateful . . . But I love Ken, I cannot help loving him! And he isn't a killer and he has come here to prove it and seek out the men who pinned the shooting on him. Oh, *please* believe me, Uncle Ben! I *know* Ken is innocent! That old man, Macky, who was shot, was coming to give evidence that would have freed Ken. He told Texas he saw who the killer was—and it wasn't Ken—and now he can never speak.' She turned her head to hide the tears that filled her eyes and heard her uncle say,

'Maybe you're right, or partly right. Your aunt believes what you say. I'm not saying more, but I won't let you get yourself involved in danger, and you've taken on a dangerous life in loving a law-dodger.'

'You won't give Ken away?'

'I don't kick a man when he's down..I'll keep an open mind, Avon, but you're not to risk meeting him again until he's cleared of this crime.'

Avon was silent. Perhaps she would never have the chance of meeting Ken again. Her uncle wanted to protect her, but if Ken died, she knew there would be nothing for her to live for.

CHAPTER
FIFTEEN

AVON spooned salt into the pan of oatmeal and turned to her aunt.

'I don't want to attend Pheelie's party, Aunt Rita.'

Rita straightened up from packing straw around a carton of eggs for market.

'I guess you'd best go, Avon. Daisy'll be right disappointed—and folks might ask questions. It will do you good to see company, you're looking right peaked, your eyes are getting bigger and your face thinner every day. I'd be happy to see you go, child, and get taken out of yourself.'

Avon sighed. 'Very well, if you wish me to go. But I have no heart for company.'

'Reckon not, when your heart's up in the hills with that sky rider.'

Daisy rode over later in the day, almost as if she suspected her friend of trying to escape the party.

'I'm real set on your coming, Avon. Things haven't been easy. Pheelie seems out of humour, she's real tetchy. I won't enjoy the party if you don't come.'

'I shall come,' Avon promised her. 'Perhaps Pheelie is missing her fiancé.'

'Well mebbe. Of course she's disappointed he can't come, he's all tied up with some important business in Boston. Ma wanted to put the party off, but Pheelie's set on it.'

It was true Avon had no heart for festivities. Her thoughts continually turned to Ken and when she would meet him again. The attack on the Indian boy, and the disappearance of her note, made her uneasy. There was weight on her heart and her nerves were tightly strung as she dressed for the Skellar party and she wished with all her heart that she need not go.

As Texas drove her up to the Skellar home she could see the bright lanterns hanging in the verandah and hear music and the voices of the guests.

'Ain't so many as I expected,' Texas remarked as he helped her down from the buggy.

'I expect it is mostly family and close friends,' she said. 'Don't be late coming for me, Texas.'

He nodded and drove off. Mrs Skellar greeted Avon as she entered the house and Daisy hurried to her side, looking relieved.

'Oh my! I had the horridest notion you wouldn't come, Avon. You're looking a mite tired these days. Come and take your wrap off. Kate Jonson's here, and the Muller girls and Frank.' She smiled as she led Avon into a bedroom. 'He's been asking when you'll come. Lucky he didn't ask it anywhere near Pheelie.'

'Daisy, I will not believe she has any interest in him now she is engaged.'

'Daisy shrugged, her smile gone. 'Pheelie's plain silly. I wouldn't say it to anyone but you, but she still hankers after Frank.'

They joined the other guests and Pheelie, resplendent in rose pink chiffon and with her golden curls piled elaborately on her head, greeted Avon with a smile that did not reach her eyes.

'I am sorry your fiancé could not be with you tonight,' Avon said, 'I am sure we all hoped to congratulate him.'

'Why he's just *so* tied up with work, people won't let him alone,' Pheelie told her gaily. 'He is in every big law case in Boston and just now it's real important he stays east.'

Avon moved away. Pheelie's manner was lively but her eyes were restless and her voice a trifle shrill as she greeted her friends. Avon was talking to Kate when she became aware of Frank at her elbow.

'Can I get you ladies some refreshment?' he asked, his eyes on Avon's averted face.

Kate giggled. 'I guess you can take Avon to the tables, I'm waiting on Hank to show up.'

Avon said hastily: 'I—I'm not hungry, thank you. I must go and speak to the Mullers.'

'I want to speak to you,' his hand closed on her arm, 'come with me.'

She hesitated, irritated by his insistence but not wishing to attract attention by refusing. She let him lead her away from the press of guests.

'Avon, I want to know if you have been secretly meeting the man, Ken Grant, who is wanted for murder in Laramie!'

She caught her breath, watching him warily. 'Why do you ask that?'

'You have been seen in the hills.' The harshness in his voice stung her. 'You cannot realise the danger of what you are doing! You think this man innocent, I know he is not. Why must you meet him? What is he to you?'

She drew a deep breath to steady her nerves before replying,

'He is a friend,' she said steadily, 'who has been unjustly accused, and I want to help him.'

'By risking your reputation—perhaps your life?' he demanded. 'You must be mad! If your aunt and uncle knew—'

'Frank, who my friends are and what I choose to do is no concern of yours.' Anger gave colour to her face and fire to her eyes.

'You are wrong. Everything that concerns you concerns me! You know my feelings. Avon,' his voice softened, 'what is this crazy notion of yours that you can prove a known killer innocent? I cannot let you take such risks. You must face the truth about this man and cease meeting him, he doesn't, he *cannot*, mean anything to you. I will protect you from him.'

She turned away abruptly, afraid her anger would spill

over, and left him to stare after her with narrowed eyes.

The evening was spoilt for her. She had been wrong to come. Fear and anger gripped her as she wondered how Frank had found out she met Ken. Possibly one of his men had seen her and Ken in the hills and the thought chilled her. She wished desperately for the evening to end but she had another hour, at least, to endure.

She accepted food, talked to people, smiled and kept up an appearance of gaiety, hardly aware of what she was doing. She could not shake off a feeling of dread, of something dark and threatening hanging over the evening despite the lively chatter and laughter. It must be her own fears, she thought, and the shock of Frank's words, that was making her so tense. She longed to be alone, to think what she must do and how she could warn Ken.

Guests began to leave but as yet there was no sign of Texas. The party had thinned to the Skellars, Avon and Frank when Pheelie cried out,

'There's a new moon tonight! We must all take a wish under it!'

'Why for sure,' Mrs Skellar said, smiling. 'We'll all wish for Pheelie's happiness. Come along outside.'

The women got wraps and joined the men outside the house. A thin silver crescent swung in the sky above them. People laughed and made their wishes and Avon, aware of Frank's burning gaze upon her, moved outside the little group, drawing her shawl around her against the chill night air.

Suddenly she raised her head, listening. Horsemen were approaching. The group was too noisy to hear the thud of hooves and faint jingle of harness.

Her eyes caught movement through the trees, then someone called,

'Hey, you got more visitors, Obie!'

They swept up to the house and pulled up with their horses snorting and stamping. Avon picked out Haskin and behind him were two men she did not know and between them, Red Jessup!

'Sorry to trouble you, Skellar,' Haskin got down stiffly from his mount. 'I'll have to borrow a couple of fresh horses, one of ours is lame and the other bushed.'

'Why for sure, Sheriff,' Mr Skellar came forward, staring at the men. 'Take your pick. You out on business?'

'Yep,' the Sheriff's voice was grim. 'We got our man.'

'I'll rustle up some coffee for you men,' Mrs Skellar said, 'you sure look wore out.'

'Thanks all the same, Ma'am, but we ain't got time. We got a prisoner to stow in jail.' He jerked his head at Jessup sitting stiffly in his saddle, his eyes, under the shadow of his hat, darting among the group. They lit and remained on Frank Carline.

'What in hell do you mean by arresting my foreman, Haskin?' Frank demanded as he strode forward. 'You've no right—'

'Reckon we've plenty right, Carline, he's a killer.'

There was a concerted indrawing of breath from the little group facing the posse. Avon was staring into the darkness. Her eyes had caught sight of two more horsemen dismounting. She must be dreaming! It could not be . . . Yes, one was Ken Grant! In the dim light she could not see his face but his head turned sharply in her direction for a second as Frank snapped,

'You're loco, Haskin, he's my foreman!'

'And he's the man who killed young Jones down in Laramie.'

'That's a damn lie!'

'That's the truth, Carline.'

'I say it isn't possible! I've known Red since—' he broke off abruptly as Ken walked out of the shadows. 'Good God, man! *There's* your killer!'

Avon, watching with her hands clasped so tightly she felt her nails dig into her flesh, saw Ken standing, tall and grim, a week's stubble on his chin and his eyes deadly as steel as he said,

'Guess again, Carline.'

'Grant's free,' the sheriff growled, 'we've proof he didn't kill Jones.'

'What proof?' Frank demanded fiercely.

Without turning his head, Haskin beckoned to a man behind him, a small withered man with a straggling beard stained with tobacco juice.

'Macky here saw the shooting and recognised Jessup.'

Frank stepped back, his face tight. 'Macky's dead!'

'No he ain't. He got a flesh wound and shammed dead and I came along before his killer rode down to make sure.' There was a grim amusement in the sheriff's voice as he went on: 'It suited me to make out he'd been killed, so certain gents could relax and take things easy.'

'But—but there was a *funeral*,' Mrs Skellar quavered in scandalised tones.

'Had to be, Ma'am, seeing Macky was dead—or supposed to be, I'll take those mounts now, Skellar—'

'*Reach for the sky*!' The order came like the crack of a whip. 'Don't move, anyone! Red, get their guns!'

Frank stood, his gun in his hand and his eyes sweeping the men before him. Slowly hands were raised, with muttered curses, while Jessup, a grin distorting his dark face, swiftly disarmed the men.

Suddenly Pheelie screamed: 'Frank! What are you doing? No—no! It *can't* be true!' She ran to him, sobbing, only to be roughly flung aside.

'Hold 'em, Red,' Frank snapped. Avon, staring in horror, saw no sign of the gentle, pleasant man she knew. Frank's face was hard steel, his mouth a thin line and his eyes evil, 'while I set the horses off.'

A shot over their heads sent the horses rearing and racing off into the dark. A few minutes later, shots and a wild stampede told the silent group the corral horses had been released, while Jessup stood, tense and watchful, with his gun threatening them.

Suddenly there was the sound of wheels approaching. For a second, Jessup's eyes flicked away from the group. In that second Ken lunged forward and smashed his fist into Jessup's jaw! As the two men crashed to the ground, the sheriff sprang forward and kicked aside the gun that had fallen from Jessup's hand.

Avon darted forward. 'Ken! Are you hurt?' He had risen, nursing a bleeding hand, while Haskin and one of his men grappled with Jessup.

'Stand away from him!'

Avon swung around and her face slowly blanched. Frank stood on the verandah steps, gun in hand. No one moved except Texas who had emerged from the dark and now moved back, one hand fumbling at his shirt. 'He's afraid . . .' Avon thought incoherently, 'I've never known Texas to be afraid . . .'

'You've got it coming to you, Grant!' Frank's voice was chill as ice and deadly as steel, 'the sky rider has run out of luck at last!'

His lips drew back in an animal snarl as he aimed at Ken. Before his finger tightened on the trigger, a shot rang out and for a second he swayed, then fell against the verandah post, gripping his chest as his gun dropped from his fingers. In stunned silence the group watched him slide slowly to the ground as the red stain spread ever wider on his white shirt.

Avon gasped: '*Texas*!' and swayed, feeling suddenly faint. Then Ken was beside her holding her as she stared at the man still gripping a smoking gun, his eyes never leaving the wounded man on the steps.

'It's all right, honey,' Ken's arm tightened around her, 'it's over.'

Abruptly all was chaos. People surged forward, shouting. Mr Skellar caught his wife as she fainted. Pheelie screamed and burst into agonised sobbing. 'Frank! Frank, my darling . . .'

'Round up the horses,' someone yelled, 'there's the two horses Frank and Jessup figured getting away on, use 'em!'

'Ken—he meant to kill you!' Avon whispered, still chilled with horror.

'Darn near did too,' Haskin had paused beside them. 'I reckon none of us knew Texas carried a shoulder gun—and sure knew how to use it. Me, I ain't asking no questions about that, he's saved me a heap of trouble—and saved your life, Grant.' He looked at them, at Ken's arm around Avon as she leaned against him and a sudden bleakness tightened his heavy face. Then he strode on to where Red Jessup was sullenly nursing a broken jaw.

'Is it really true, Ken that you are free now?' She looked up at him, at the lean, haggard face of the man she loved and would always love.

He nodded, smiling wryly. 'Haskin suspected it was a framed killing, that's why he didn't hunt me too hard. He was out for bigger game, rustlers and lawbreakers, the Blackface gang, Frank's gang.'

'*Frank*? You mean—'

'I mean Frank Carline is the brain behind all these crimes in the territory. He's been clever, darn clever, but he slipped up when he sent Red Jessup down to Laramie to kill Jones who was threatening to split on him.'

'But Ken, didn't you see Jessup in the saloon that night?'

He shook his head. 'The poker players were in a corner with hats pulled down low. I didn't take notice of them.' He picked her up in his arms. 'You're going home, honey. You've had enough shocks for one night I reckon.' He carried her over to the buggy and stooping, kissed her hard and swiftly before putting her in the seat. 'I'll call Texas.'

But Texas shook his head. 'Sheriff says I'm to ride with him to town. Drive her to the farm, Grant. You can have my bunk for the night. Reckon I'll be along sometime tomorrow—if I'm not in jail.'

'Suits me fine.' Ken climbed in beside Avon and shook the reins.

For a while, as they drove through the starlit night, Avon was silent. Ken's arm was around her holding her close and the happiness filling her heart was enough for the moment. But after a time she raised her head to ask,

'Did you suspect Frank?'

'Not at first. But your recognising the train robber, and something shifty about Jessup, put me onto the trail and I guessed there was bad work going on and meant to smoke it out. Once I'd seen Jessup come out of that rock face—and taken a look in there myself—I knew I was near getting the truth. I guess Haskin was riding the same trail; he'd had his eye on Carline but couldn't get anything on him until Macky let out he'd seen Jessup in Laramie.'

'But how did that lead him to know Frank was leader of the gang?'

'All the poker-players were Carline's men, Macky recognised them. And the barkeep cracked wide open under Haskin's questioning. He'd been bribed plenty to lay me out with a bottle and swear I'd shot Jones, and he was scared to his bones of what they'd do to him if he didn't play their game.'

'Frank tried to make me think the sheriff was rustling cattle,' she told him, 'and I almost believed him. Ken, is Frank badly wounded?'

'The shot got him in the chest and he didn't look good, Avon.'

She shivered. 'He was going to shoot you in cold blood! He knew I had been meeting you; he must have seen the message the Indian boy carried. He frightened me tonight! I saw how he hated you.'

'He got windy when he knew I'd located his hole-up, and when he heard Haskin had sent word by the Indians that I was in the clear. Haskin was darn smart in putting out Macky had passed in his chips, though maybe the preacher won't take kindly to knowing he buried a coffin full of brick. It made Carline think himself safe—and gave Haskin time to ride to Laramie and shake the truth from the barkeep.'

She leant against his shoulder. 'I don't understand

about Texas. He said he couldn't use a gun.'

Ken grinned. 'The old devil! He toted an ace in the hole—that's a shoulder holster you don't see. I'd like to know how long he's worn it. I guess he's reasons for playing helpless where guns are concerned. Darned lucky for me he used it so prompt.'

'If Frank had killed you . . . Oh Ken, I could not have lived without you!'

'You won't have to, sweetheart. You'll be Mrs Ken Grant, bossing your husband and my Uncle Jake down in South Dakota. I guess he's had a scare, me disappearing like that.'

Rita and Ben were on the steps when Ken drove up.

'Mercy, child, what delayed you—' Rita began, then she saw Ken and her eyes widened. 'What's happened? Is he . . .'

Ben stepped forward, his eyes stern. 'I've seen your face on a poster. What are you doing here?'

'Driving me home.' Avon let Ken swing her down from her seat. 'It is all right, Uncle Ben, Ken is free and the sheriff has the real killer, Ken will tell you.'

It was after midnight before it was all told and talked over. Rita brewed coffee and sat listening, her eyes on Avon's glowing face. At last she said,

'Well, I never did have a liking for Frank Carline. He's been mightly clever, it's a pity he don't turn his brains to honest use. How come he knew how to organise crime so handy?'

Ken finished his coffee. 'Born with it, I reckon. When Haskin got suspicious, he checked Carline's record in England and it wasn't good. He'd plenty of reasons to get out of that country and try his luck out West.'

'Seems he'll be buried out West too,' Ben spoke grimly and his eyes were hard. 'Men like him aren't wanted here—and don't last long. I'm glad you're cleared, Grant—and I think Avon is, too.'

'She's too whacked to know what she thinks right now,' Rita said firmly. 'Come, child, I'll help you to bed.

Now quit hanging on to your sky rider, he'll be here tomorrow. You can dream of that ranch in South Dakota.' She put her arm about Avon and led her away. 'Though I'm no friend of his now he's taking you from us.'

'South Dakota is not all that far away,' Ken smiled at her as she rose from the table. 'If Ben ever feels he'd want to move farms, I reckon Uncle Jake could sell him land, and good farming land at that.'

Ben nodded slowly, his eyes following the women. 'I might, at that.'

'Now, Texas,' Avon sat down beside him on the tree stump outside the back porch, 'you are going to tell me if you knew Macky was alive, and why you said you couldn't use a gun, and why—'

'Aw gee, Avon, I'm all wore out with questions! Haskin don't ask too many, but the population of Sweetwater is just too darn curious for my taste.' He squirted a stream of tobacco juice at a passing chicken. 'So don't *you* ride the same trail.'

'Texas, I must know! *Did* you know—'

'Hell, yes, I knowed about Macky, Haskin told me and told me to keep my mouth shut about it. *Now* will you quit drilling me with them big eyes of yours!'

'But your gun, Texas; you told me . . .' She paused, arrested by something in his battered face. He had raised his head and was staring at the hills but she knew he was not seeing them.

'I killed a man once . . . I kept out of gun fights after that.'

'But you carried a shoulder gun.'

He looked at her then. 'I didn't aim to use it 'less it were plumb necessary—like last night. Frank sure meant to rub out Ken.'

'You saved him, Texas. Is Frank . . . Will he . . .'

'Died afore they got him to Sweetwater.' Texas took out his plug of dark, rank tobacco and cut a lump off it.

'Saved Haskin the trouble of hanging him. Jessup's set for a necktie party, and maybe some of the others as have been rounded up. One of 'em has passed in his chips already, the man with the scar face you recognised. He's been found with a Sioux arrow through him.'

Avon drew in a sharp breath. 'I think I know why.' Seeing Eye had taken his revenge.

Ken rode into Sweetwater next day on Blazer and Texas rode with him. When Ken returned he was on Darkie and leading Blazer. Rita had supper ready and she and Ben sedulously avoided the verandah after the meal.

'I'm coming back for you as soon as I've fixed up with Uncle Jake,' Ken murmured as he held her in his arms. 'You hussle up the preacher, I don't aim to wait a minute more than I must to get myself settled with a wife. Are you happy, Avon girl?'

'Oh Ken, you must know just how happy I am! If Frank had shot you . . .'

'We'll forget all that, honey. What about your folks in England?'

'My folks are Uncle Ben and Aunt Rita,' she told him, reaching up to kiss him. 'My home is here—and so is my heart!'

How to join in a whole new world of romance

It's very easy to subscribe to the Mills & Boon Reader Service. As a regular reader, you can enjoy a whole range of special benefits. Bargain offers. Big cash savings. Your own free Reader Service newsletter, packed with knitting patterns, recipes, competitions, and exclusive book offers.

We send you the very latest titles each month, postage and packing free – no hidden extra charges. There's absolutely no commitment – you receive books for only as long as you want.

We'll send you details. Simply send the coupon – or drop us a line for details about the Mills & Boon Reader Service Subscription Scheme. Post to: Mills & Boon Reader Service, P.O. Box 236, Thornton Road, Croydon, Surrey CR9 3RU, England. *Please note: READERS IN SOUTH AFRICA please write to: Mills & Boon Reader Service of Southern Africa, Private Bag X3010, Randburg 2125, S. Africa.

Please send me details of the Mills & Boon Subscription Scheme.

NAME (Mrs/Miss) _____ EP3

ADDRESS _____

COUNTY/COUNTRY_____ POST/ZIP CODE_____

BLOCK LETTERS, PLEASE

Mills & Boon
the rose of romance